WINDS OF DANGER

LANTERN BEACH ROMANTIC SUSPENSE,
BOOK 4

CHRISTY BARRITT

River Heights

COMPLETE BOOK LIST

Squeaky Clean Mysteries:

#1 Hazardous Duty

#2 Suspicious Minds

#2.5 It Came Upon a Midnight Crime (novella)

#3 Organized Grime

#4 Dirty Deeds

#5 The Scum of All Fears

#6 To Love, Honor and Perish

#7 Mucky Streak

#8 Foul Play

#9 Broom & Gloom

#10 Dust and Obey

#11 Thrill Squeaker

#11.5 Swept Away (novella)

#12 Cunning Attractions

#13 Cold Case: Clean Getaway

#14 Cold Case: Clean Sweep

While You Were Sweeping, A Riley Thomas Spinoff

The Sierra Files:

#1 Pounced

#2 Hunted

#3 Pranced

#4 Rattled

#5 Caged (coming soon)

The Gabby St. Claire Diaries (a Tween Mystery series):

The Curtain Call Caper

The Disappearing Dog Dilemma

The Bungled Bike Burglaries

The Worst Detective Ever

#1 Ready to Fumble

#2 Reign of Error

#3 Safety in Blunders

#4 Join the Flub

#5 Blooper Freak

#6 Flaw Abiding Citizen

#7 Gaffe Out Loud

Shadow of Intrigue

Storm of Doubt

Lantern Beach P.D.

On the Lookout

Attempt to Locate

First Degree Murder

Dead on Arrival

Plan of Action

Carolina Moon Series

Home Before Dark

Gone By Dark

Wait Until Dark

Light the Dark

Taken By Dark

Suburban Sleuth Mysteries:

Death of the Couch Potato's Wife

Fog Lake Suspense:

Edge of Peril

Margin of Error

Cape Thomas Series:

Dubiosity

Disillusioned

Distorted

Standalone Romantic Mystery:

The Good Girl

Suspense:

Imperfect

The Wrecking

Standalone Romantic-Suspense:

Keeping Guard

The Last Target

Race Against Time

Ricochet

Key Witness

Lifeline

High-Stakes Holiday Reunion

Desperate Measures

Hidden Agenda

Mountain Hideaway

Dark Harbor

Shadow of Suspicion

The Baby Assignment

The Cradle Conspiracy

Nonfiction:

Characters in the Kitchen

Changed: True Stories of Finding God through Christian Music (out of print)

The Novel in Me: The Beginner's Guide to Writing and Publishing a Novel (out of print)

CHAPTER ONE

WES O'NEILL SHOVED his paddle into the water and glanced at Paige Henderson across the glassy surface of the Pamlico Sound. She stood on her paddleboard, her lithe figure illuminated by the glowing horizon. The woman made using the SUP look as effortless as walking down the street.

"You're pretty good at this," Wes pushed his sunglasses up higher on his nose as the sun glared against the water.

"And you're surprised?" Paige raised an eyebrow and paddled closer to him, gliding across the water with a mischievous glint in her eyes.

Wes halfway expected her to say, "Let's race." Instead, she grinned at him, the picture of the whole-some girl next door.

"Surprised is a strong word," he finally said. "Most people don't do this well their first time out."

"Well, I'm a natural. What can I say?" As if to prove it, Paige balanced on one leg and stretched her other leg and arm out parallel to each other, like a ballerina warming up before a performance.

"Showoff."

She glanced over her shoulder. "Your turn."

Wes pictured himself trying that pose and snorted. "Only if you want to see me end up in the water."

She flashed another grin. "Maybe."

"It would bring you too much satisfaction."

This woman had fascinated him since they'd first met, and Wes couldn't pinpoint why. On one hand, there were so many reasons. Paige was smart, beautiful, personable. She was unassuming, cute, athletic.

On the other hand, Wes had been immune to the lure of the opposite sex for a long time now. He hadn't ever seen himself becoming romantically interested in someone again. Not after his last relationship and the string of events that happened afterward.

Then Paige had shown up here in Lantern Beach, with her corkscrew honey-blonde curls, toothy smile, and freckled skin. Something had begun to slowly change inside him. He felt a new stirring. He felt . . . hope.

Maybe it was because Paige seemed different from the other women he'd met in the past couple years. She had so much life and love inside her that he just wanted to know everything about her.

They'd been hanging out for the last month and getting to know each other. Despite that, one part of Wes still wanted to hold Paige at arm's length. If only he could undo the mistakes of his past. But those choices still tainted his future.

"There's a storm coming across the Pamlico." Wes nodded across the miles and miles of open water to the west. "We should get back. These systems can come up fast around here, and we don't want to get caught in it."

She followed his gaze. "That storm is a long way away. I think you just don't want me to show you up." Her voice held a humor-filled challenge, and she danced a little jig on the board—without falling off.

And that was just another reason the woman fascinated him.

"What do you know about storms?" he asked. Her statement had sounded authoritative.

"My father was a fisherman. I grew up on the water." A wistfulness floated through her voice, hinting at secrets that she wasn't ready to share.

She kept so many details of her past private, alluding to hurts too painful to speak about. Maybe they were both finally starting to open up, although Wes had to admit that there was a certain comfort in this phase of simply enjoying each other's company.

"So, your dad was a fisherman, but you've never been paddleboarding?" Wes tried to keep his voice light.

"Paddleboarding is for the hoity-toity types. I grew up around real watermen, people who made their living by harvesting the treasures of the ocean."

He let out a low whistle "I see how it is. Sorry to make you do something fancy."

She shrugged. "Maybe I've always secretly wanted to try—I just didn't want to be judged for it."

"Now the truth comes out."

She stuck her paddle in the water and splashed it. Brackish liquid sprayed across his face. Wes attempted to splash her back, but his paddleboard wobbled, nearly sending him into the water.

Paige laughed with delight.

They paddled toward the shore, only stopping when the tips of their boards hit the sandy shoreline they'd launched from two hours ago. Wes operated his side business from this area during the summer. The soundside beach wasn't far from the lighthouse. This part of the island was surrounded by the dense, shrubby maritime forest that hugged a patch of sand.

When Wes did his tours, he brought in a trailer loaded with kayaks and paddleboards and set up a temporary site to launch from. Since he didn't own the land, he had to have a portable setup. The town did allow him to use a small parking area at the end of the sandy trail leading here.

Summertime had just arrived, and he was gearing up for a busy season. Paige had requested a personal tour of the area, and Wes had no good reason to object. In fact, he'd looked forward to showing her his favorite little coves.

Paige gracefully stepped onto the shore and grabbed her board, holding it to her side and looking like she could grace a magazine cover as the water sparkled behind her. "What next?"

Wes let out a laugh and pulled his own board onto the sand. "Next? You're ready for more?"

"Hey, I paid for a three-hour tour." Her eyes glimmered with humor. "We're only two hours in."

Wes left his board on the shore and stepped closer. Close enough to see the flecks of gold in her eyes. To smell her coconut-scented sunscreen. To feel the invisible pull she had on him. "You paid?"

She raised her shoulders playfully. "I mean, if making dinner for you for two nights is considered payment, then yes. And, if I recall correctly, that was our deal. You may have gotten the short end of the stick, however, since my spaghetti with meat sauce was runny, and I forgot to add chili powder to my tacos."

He'd noticed. But, like a smart man, he hadn't complained.

As he stared at her smiling face, he sucked in a quick breath.

Paige was so beautiful. Everything in Wes told him to step closer. To tell her how he was feeling. To forget all the reasons he shouldn't move forward with the relationship.

What was wrong with him? He should know better than to get close. But that didn't stop his heart from feeling the connection he sensed with Paige. It was like this woman could easily be his best friend and soulmate wrapped into one.

He cleared his throat, not ready to take the next step but not ready to say goodbye either. "Maybe we could . . . get some ice cream instead?"

Her smile slipped just slightly. "It's a deal."

You know what? He was being stupid. He shouldn't let the past hold him back like this. If he had feelings for Paige, he should tell her. Show her.

As he tried to find his voice, he reached for her arm. "Paige—"

Before he could finish, he heard something move in the distance and jerked his gaze toward the sound.

What was that? It had almost looked like . . . he shook his head. No, he was just seeing things. It couldn't have been. Not here. Not now.

"Wes?" Paige followed his gaze and glanced over her shoulder.

He didn't say anything. Instead, he paced toward the sound. Had he been imagining things or had he seen a flash of movement? Almost like a person had been hiding behind the thick foliage, watching them.

In fact, it almost looked like . . .

No, the feelings Wes had for Paige had stirred up things inside him, played with his thoughts, his mind. Women had a tendency to do that.

Yet he had to be sure.

"Stay here," he muttered.

Each step felt heavy with anticipation as he continued toward the woods. He dodged some undergrowth on the edge of the forest as he squeezed past some trees.

But the shadow was gone. No one was here. Only trees and bushes and marsh grass.

He scanned his surroundings once more, looking for footprints or some other sign to indicate he wasn't seeing things, wasn't being paranoid.

He bent down. The brush was slightly trampled right here.

He moved the undergrowth to check if a footprint could be seen beneath it. There was no print. Instead, he found little white petals. Daisy petals.

Daisies . . . Jennifer's favorite flower.

His heart pulsed in his ears at a dizzying tempo.

"Wes, what is it?" Paige appeared behind him, a concerned expression on her face.

Wes pressed his lips shut and stood. What did he even tell her?

There was nothing he could say, he realized. There was no way he could tell Paige that he thought he'd seen his crazy ex-girlfriend out there hiding between the trees. That these petals could be evidence she'd been here.

The ex-girlfriend who was off-balance enough to go to drastic measures. The ex-girlfriend who'd caused him to escape here to Lantern Beach, North Carolina, in order to get away from her antics. Her threats. Her obsession.

Had Jennifer found him here?

Wes swallowed hard. Because, if she had, his future suddenly wasn't looking so bright. Nor was any possibility of a relationship with Paige.

CHAPTER TWO

AGAINST HIS OWN DESIRE, Wes canceled on having ice cream with Paige. He told her that something had come up that couldn't wait. He'd seen the questions in her eyes, but they were questions he couldn't answer yet. Maybe not ever.

Instead, he dropped her off, a new heaviness surrounding him as he said goodbye. He went back to his cottage and pulled up his computer.

He stared at the screen a moment, his fingers refusing to cooperate and type.

He was probably imagining things. He probably hadn't seen Jennifer today. She'd moved on. Probably found love—and obsession—with some other poor, unsuspecting soul. It had been three years, after all.

Those daisy petals . . . maybe they'd been from

some other plant. Or a weed. Or . . . there were other explanations. Right?

His lungs felt frozen as he forced his fingers into action. He typed Jennifer's name into the Facebook search bar.

Her picture appeared on the screen. She smiled, her glossy blonde hair falling neatly below her shoulders. Her blue eyes danced with life. Her smile was bright—almost too bright.

Wes had first been drawn to those qualities. She'd been pretty and approachable and engaging. She'd been great at hiding the darker side of herself and putting her best foot forward. That was what made her so unsettling.

He scanned Jennifer's most recent posts. It appeared she still lived in Virginia Beach. Her work history showed that, in the past three years, she'd worked as a receptionist at a car dealership, as an assistant at a nursing home, and as an admissions counselor at a small college.

All in three years. That sounded right. She'd always had a hard time holding down a job.

Because she was unstable.

Uncountable pictures of Jennifer smiling with people filled her page. No doubt these were mostly new friends. She couldn't maintain friendships any more than she could hold down a job. But, to look at the photos, she seemed so effervescent.

Yet, beneath that façade, she'd been off-balance. Needy. Jealous.

And dangerous.

He looked at the date of her most recent post. Two weeks ago. Since then, nothing. Before that, she'd easily had two or three posts a day.

It could be because the two of them weren't friends on social media, so maybe Wes couldn't see all her posts. His own account was set to private. Even his business listings . . . they contained only a business name and not his name.

He didn't want Jennifer to find him again. Ever.

But what if she had?

Wes sighed and leaned back, frowning as he stared at the screen.

The truth was that he thought someone had been watching him the past two weeks. He'd brushed it off, figuring the feeling was nothing.

One morning, his truck felt different, like someone had been inside. Again, Wes told himself he was paranoid.

But what if he wasn't? What if Jennifer had found him? She could be spinning her deadly web right now, just waiting for him to get caught in her trap.

He ran a hand over his face, feeling the tension there.

What was he going to do? Was he reading too much into this?

A knock sounded behind him, and Wes nearly jumped out of his chair. He turned and saw his best friend's face through the glass pane at the top of his door.

Ty Chambers was a former Navy SEAL, husband of the town's police chief, and director of the Hope House, a nonprofit organization that served veterans. He'd also been Wes's most trusted confidante since Wes had moved to Lantern Beach.

But even Ty didn't know about Jennifer. Wes had only wanted to forget about the woman. Maybe that had been his first mistake.

He'd let down his guard.

Ty's timing was good—Wes could use a sounding board right now. He swung open the door.

"Hey, man." Wes ran a hand over his shaved head, feeling more out of sorts than he would like.

"I figured you'd be hanging out with Paige again."

After shaking the rain from his jacket, Ty stepped into the entry. That storm on the horizon now raged outside. Wes had been right to get off the water when he did. Thunder rumbled in the distance.

"I saw your truck here, so I decided to swing by," Ty continued. "I was hoping to borrow that nail gun. Mine stopped working."

"Yeah, I can definitely get that for you." But he made no effort to move.

"So, where's Paige?" Ty glanced behind Wes, into the living room. "You two have been inseparable lately."

His stomach clenched. "We went paddleboarding earlier, but with the storm coming our way, we called it quits."

Ty studied him a moment and crossed his arms, an air of suspicion around him. "Everything okay?"

"Yeah, man. Why?" Wes took a step back, giving one more glance at his computer screen. Jennifer's face still smiled at him from the monitor. Just seeing it caused dread to drip down his spine.

"You just have that look, like something is bothering you."

He contemplated his response for a moment before sitting down a little too hard in his computer chair. He was having second thoughts about sharing too much. "I'd tell you, but you'll think I'm crazy."

"Try me." Ty lowered himself into a nearby armchair. "I know all about crazy."

After the ordeal Ty had been through recently, Wes knew his friend told the truth. A cult had been taken down on the island, but not without collateral damage. Damage that included Ty being abducted and . . .

Wes paused his thoughts. He still couldn't stomach the idea of everything that had happened in this peaceful little community or how close his friend had come to dying. In the end, the ordeal had made them all stronger. Pulled them closer together. Solidified them as islanders.

"There are a few things you don't know about my life before I came here to Lantern Beach." Wes felt his gaze cloud over as memories filled his mind.

"Like what?"

He drew in a deep breath. "Well, you know I was in Virginia Beach prior to coming here."

"That's right. You've mentioned that a few times."

"The truth is I was in a toxic relationship with a woman who . . . well, I don't know a nice way to say this except to put it out there. She was crazy. Certifiably."

Ty narrowed his eyes. "Define 'crazy.' Did she try to kill you or something?"

"To kill me? No. But she tried to hurt anyone she perceived as a threat. Any women." Wes felt like he'd been punched in the gut as he said the words, as memories filled him. He'd feared for the safety of those women—innocent women who did nothing more than go on a date with him.

Their lives had been turned upside down as a result. One had become the recipient of a string of nasty text messages. Another had gotten sick when someone put eyedrops in her water. Another had been stalked, which scared her to the point of sleeping with a gun at night. Each incident had escalated.

Paige's sweet image flashed through his mind. She was better off if Wes stayed away. His absence was the best thing he could do for her.

Even if it killed him.

Because anything was better than Paige being hurt . . . at least until he knew for sure what was going on.

But he prayed that Jennifer hadn't found him. Because his whole life would be turned inside out if she had.

CHAPTER THREE

THE NEXT MORNING, Paige stared at the phone in front of her, willing it to ring. Willing work to drop in her lap. Nothing was worse than doing nothing.

Doing nothing left her alone with her thoughts. Her regrets. Her insecurities. That was only one of the reasons she tried so hard to stay busy. She needed to ease the ache in her heart.

She'd taken this job here at the Lantern Beach Police Department when she came into town a month ago. Since she'd worked as a dispatcher for Fish and Wildlife down in Florida, she was well-qualified.

When she'd arrived, the island had been in the middle of a crisis and the action nonstop. In the month since everything blew up, the calls had slowed to a crawl. Which she should welcome. That meant crime had dissipated. That was good, right?

But as a receptionist and dispatcher, that also meant long, boring days.

At least she'd had Wes to distract her. He'd been a very nice distraction—one that she'd dreamed about having in her future for a long time.

Wes . . . she leaned back in her seat as his face filled her mind. The edges of her lips pulled down in a frown.

From the moment Paige had met Wes, she'd known something was different about him. The man had a killer smile and eyes that were always laced with a mischievous glint. He'd fascinated her and pulled her heart in directions she hadn't anticipated.

However, she hadn't come here looking for romance. No, she'd come here to beat herself up for her past mistakes. To figure out where she'd gone so wrong in life. To wade through the murky waters of her soul and figure out if she could forgive herself.

Wes hadn't been part of the plan.

She frowned as she remembered how yesterday had ended. Wes had gotten all weird. What had happened to cause his change of heart?

Things had gone from playful with talks of spending more time together to as freezing cold as that ice cream they were supposed to get.

Had Paige said something? Done something?

Men . . . would she ever figure them out?

No. Definitely, no.

It was probably just as well. She had terrible taste in men. As memories of the mistakes she'd made in her last relationship filled her mind, Paige held back her tears. If only she could go back . . . she'd change things. She wouldn't have fallen under Owen's spell. Wouldn't have made the same life-changing choices.

But she couldn't go back. She only knew she could never make those same mistakes again. No man was worth what she'd lost.

She straightened her posture as she snapped back to reality.

She had work to do.

Paige glanced at her desk. She'd already straightened the papers in all her files. She'd lined up the paperclips so they were all facing the same direction. She'd tested every ink pen and gotten rid of any that didn't work.

If only she could order her life as easily as she organized office supplies.

"Hey, Paige."

She looked up and saw the police chief step through the front door. Since Paige had worked here, she'd found Chief Cassidy Chambers to be refreshing and kind—but Paige also knew she didn't want to cross the woman. Chief Chambers had been a strong, tough leader here on the island, the type of woman little girls wanted to be like when they grew up.

"Morning, Chief Chambers." Paige plastered on a pleasant smile, forgetting her personal struggles in an effort to be professional. More than anything, she wanted to do a good job. To make someone proud. To undo the damage she'd done back home in Florida.

The chief paused and leaned against the counter. Her wavy blonde hair cascaded over her shoulders. Paige knew that before her boss took any calls, the woman would pull her hair into a neat, professional bun. Until then, she looked relaxed, like a lifeguard in a police uniform.

"Any calls this morning?" Chief Chambers grabbed a mint from the little glass bowl on the counter and began unwrapping it.

Paige shook her head and stared at her blank notepad. "No, nothing. Not even a cat up a tree. No fender benders. No missing beach equipment."

"Well, I'd say that was good." She popped the peppermint into her mouth. The chief had told her one time that talking to people with coffee breath should be a crime within itself, revealing a humorous side.

"Me too."

"Everything good to go for the beach cleanup efforts at the end of the week?"

It was a project Chief Chambers had asked Paige to oversee, which was perfect since she was passionate about keeping the ocean clean. Wes had also volunteered to help her.

Her gut twisted. Would he still do that? She wasn't sure.

Paige remembered the chief's question and cleared her throat. "Everything is great for the Lantern Beach Scrub a Dub Dub. Now we just need to hope for good weather."

Paige had come up with the name and game plan for the event. On Friday, volunteers would gather to clean the shoreline around the island, all the way from the public beaches to the lesser-known shorelines on the sound.

"So far, one hundred people have signed up to help," Paige continued. "A couple have volunteered to come out with scuba gear, so we'll actually be in the water as well. By the time peak season hits, this place will be pristine."

"Perfect." The chief lingered near the reception desk. "Look, I'm having some people over to my place tonight. Do you want to come?"

Paige felt her chest well with excitement—and then quickly deflate. The thought of hanging out with the chief and her friends sounded so nice. But Paige felt like things were strained between her and

Wes. Certainly, he would be there. After all, Wes was best friends with the chief's husband, Ty.

Paige frowned, knowing what her answer needed to be. "I would, but I don't think that's a great idea."

The chief tilted her head in confusion. "Why's that?"

How much should she say? After all, the chief was her boss, not a friend. Yet, Paige desperately wanted someone to talk to. She hadn't really formed any female friendships since she'd moved here—she had no one to blame for that but herself. She'd struggled with deep relationships over the past couple years.

"Wes and I . . . I don't know." Paige shrugged. "I'm not sure what happened yesterday, but he cut our plans short, dropped me off, and I haven't heard from him since. I don't want to read too much into things but . . . I just feel like something has changed. Call it women's intuition."

The chief let out a soft, curious grunt. "Really? Nothing happened before that?"

"No. We had a great time paddleboarding. Then we got out of the water, talked about getting ice cream. He looked into the distance like he saw a ghost, and then it was like he turned into a different person. He mumbled some kind of excuse and dropped me off at home." Paige clamped her mouth shut. She hadn't intended on saying so much.

A knot formed between Chief Chambers' eyes. "That doesn't sound like Wes."

Paige shrugged. She'd gotten too close too fast. She shouldn't be feeling this defeated at this point in their undefined relationship.

"Easy come, easy go, right?" She tried to sound like she wasn't bothered, when, in truth, she was. Very bothered.

Chief Chambers twisted her head in a quick shake. "You don't understand. Wes . . . well, I don't think anything about his connection with you has been easy for him. For as long as I've known him, no one has ever turned his head."

Paige's heart lifted—even though she willed it not to. She didn't want the chief's words to thrill her like they did. "Is that right?"

"Women here on the island—the single ones— they fake plumbing emergencies just so Wes will come out to their place."

Paige resisted a smile. She could easily see that. Wes had this rugged kind of manliness about him. Plus he was playful and hardworking. He liked keeping up with current events, and he was surprisingly perceptive. He made an intriguing package.

"How does Wes handle that?" Paige asked, honestly curious.

"Like a gentleman. He does his work and gets out. That doesn't stop some women from continuing to call him." Chief Chambers let out a chuckle before turning serious again. "All that said, Wes isn't someone who uses women . . . I don't know. He's seemed very content being single for as long as I've known him."

"I see." Paige wished she had more to say, but words failed her. Maybe Wes had just changed his mind about her . . . for no apparent reason. Or maybe he loved his singleness so much that he'd decided to stay with that status. It shouldn't matter this much to Paige. It wasn't like the two of them were official. They'd never even kissed. Why couldn't she just shrug it off instead of feeling so torn?

"Just give him some time. I don't know what's going on, but that doesn't sound like the Wes I know."

Maybe Paige shouldn't give up on him yet. Besides, she'd just come from one bad relationship. The last thing she wanted was to jump into another. Some space and distance would be good.

Just as the thought entered Paige's head, her phone buzzed. She looked down and saw it was a message from Wes. Her heart lifted before crashing again.

She read the words there again.

I'm sorry, Paige. I'm not going to be able to help with the beach cleanup project this weekend. Sorry to let you know this way, but something has come up that can't be changed.

Her intuition was correct. Something had definitely changed between them, leaving her reeling with confusion and disappointment.

———

WES PULLED his trailer of kayaks and paddleboards up to the sandy beach. He'd finished a long day of plumbing jobs, and now he wanted to do his fun job and act as a tour guide.

He had a full schedule tonight, and he looked forward to staying busy—mostly so he could keep his mind occupied.

As he put his truck in park, he frowned. He'd hated sending Paige that text earlier today. He knew if he saw her face-to-face, he wouldn't be able to call it off. One look from her, and Wes would be back where he started—totally infatuated.

The best thing he could do right now was to keep his distance and encourage her to do the same.

He frowned as he climbed out of his truck. The only thing he could do right now was get to work.

He grabbed a clipboard to review who'd signed up for tonight's expedition. He expected people would start arriving in about thirty minutes. He'd need that time to pull the kayaks out, organize the lifejackets, and make sure everyone had signed their waivers.

He normally hired some college kids to help him, but he had another week before they would arrive. In the meantime, his friend Austin was giving him a hand today.

As if on cue, Austin pulled in behind him and hopped from his truck, wearing board shorts and a water shirt.

"Hey, hey, man!" Austin gave him a high five. "What's happening?"

"Just getting everything ready. Thanks for helping me out."

"Any time."

Austin walked with him to the trailer.

"Let's start by unloading these," Wes said. "We have twelve people signed up tonight."

"Excellent. Based on the clouds I'm seeing, it's going to be a beautiful sunset. You'll have some happy customers."

"That's what I want." Wes released one of the

straps that kept the kayaks in place. "Happy customers mean happy reviews. Happy reviews keep me in business."

They chatted as they unloaded. Austin was a contractor, and, in his free time, he and his fiancé, Skye, had been working on flipping a house. The place was nearly completed, and Wes couldn't wait to see how it looked. The normal conversation was a welcoming, albeit temporary, distraction.

"By the way, you and Skye set a date yet?" Wes asked.

Austin grinned. "We're working on it. We'd like to finish this house first."

"You better hurry up then."

Austin laughed. "I'm trying. Believe me."

Finally, all the kayaks were lined up on the shore and ready to go.

As Wes started back toward his truck to grab the life jackets, he paused and glanced down.

He leaned closer to one of the kayaks. Was that a . . . ?

"What is it, man?" Austin peered down beside him.

Wes ran his finger across the molded plastic. "It looks like there's a hole in the side of my kayak."

Austin squinted as he inspected it "Man, you're

right. Almost like someone took a drill and put it there on purpose."

A bad feeling began brewing in Wes's gut.

He hadn't seen Jennifer since he thought he'd spied her yesterday. He'd hoped he made the whole thing up, that he hadn't really seen her at all. But that was looking less like the case.

Silently, he walked to another kayak and inspected it also.

Sure enough, a hole had been drilled in this one also.

He straightened and ran a hand over his face as he squeezed his eyes shut.

This couldn't be happening. Without his kayaks, he had no tours. He had no side business.

Austin continued down the line and checked each of the kayaks. When he came back over, a grim look lined his face.

"They all have holes," he said.

His words didn't surprise Wes. That was what he'd suspected.

Jennifer must have done this. It was the only thing that made sense.

She'd sabotaged his equipment. Was it an act of revenge for rejecting her? For coming here to Lantern Beach and giving attention to another woman?

The thought of it caused unease to jostle inside him.

So much for those happy customer reviews. Wes was going to have to cancel tonight's trip and refund everyone's money.

Then he was going to have to figure out how to proceed.

CHAPTER FOUR

PAIGE NEEDED to find something to do with herself tonight after work. Normally, she'd spend her evening with Wes.

Maybe that had been her first mistake. She'd put all her eggs in one basket, so to speak. Instead of taking the time to develop other friendships, she'd been content to hang out with Wes. Story of her life.

Now that he was no longer interested in spending time with her, Paige felt lost. Then again, maybe she was reading too much into this. It had only been a day since they'd last spoken. Still, they'd talked often. Texted multiple times a day. Hung out every spare moment.

And now nothing. She'd been in enough bad relationships to see the writing on the wall.

As she pulled up to her RV, she put her beat-up

sedan in Park. She'd found a little camper to rent for the summer. It wasn't fancy or big, but it was cheaper than trying to find a house in the area.

This was no ordinary RV lot, however. Unlike many campgrounds, this little community was full of permanent island residents who couldn't afford the area's real estate prices. Cost of living and affordable housing for full-timers was always an issue in vacation towns like this one.

Wes's friend Skye had recommended the place to Paige. In fact, Skye had a retro RV a few rows down from Paige's temporary accommodation.

Paige's place wasn't much, but it was clean and sufficient. She just hated to come back here tonight with nothing to do. Nothing to do meant she had too much time to think, to rehash her regrets.

Feeling a surge of determination, she raised her chin. She would find something to do. She'd put on her suit and go down to the beach by herself, if she had to. She was not going to plan her life around a man again. She'd already made that mistake once, and it had cost her dearly.

Her heart pounded at the thought.

Her choice had been more than a mistake. It had been a decision that wreaked heartbreak and remorse. Something she could never undo. The biggest regret of her life.

Paige shook back the memories as she climbed the makeshift deck to her front door. She paused by the entrance as something on the ground caught her eye. She leaned down and picked up a bouquet of daisies that had been left there.

Daisies? Hmm.

She opened a card that had been left with them.

From a secret admirer.

A secret admirer?

Who could this be? Suddenly, her night seemed a little more interesting.

Was this Wes's way of apologizing while trying to remain mysterious? She didn't know.

But she was going to wait and see if Wes followed these up with a phone call. She didn't want to assume things. But a spark of hope lit inside her.

Maybe she'd misread the situation. Maybe Wes hadn't suddenly ended contact with her with no explanation. But, even if that was true, she needed to remain cautious.

For her heart's sake.

———

"SO YOU'RE TELLING me that someone purposefully put these holes in your kayaks?" Cassidy knelt on the sand near Wes's equipment and examined the marks, a frown on her face.

"That's correct," Wes said. "Look at the holes—they're all even and equal. It looks like someone took a drill and put these here."

Dealing with the damage was stressful enough within itself. Add to that the fact that he had to fend off angry complaints from the customers he had to cancel on . . . his day sure hadn't gone as he'd planned. He'd even sent Austin home, knowing his friend had better things to do than sit around for this.

Now Wes had to explain what had happened for the official police report. He would need one when he filed an insurance claim—something he probably should do, and quickly.

Cassidy stood and wiped the sand from her pants. "Why would someone do something like this? It's not like there are other kayaking businesses here on the island who'd have motive for shutting you down. So what's going on?"

Wes let out a long breath, contemplating what to tell her. There was no need to hide the truth. Cassidy would probably find out anyway.

He crossed his arms, the words burning his throat before they ever left his lips. "The truth is, I'm afraid one of my ex-girlfriends is in town. She's . . . scary and vengeful, and I wouldn't put something like this past her."

Cassidy narrowed her eyes as she observed him. "That's why you've been giving Paige the cold shoulder today, isn't it?"

His eyes widened with surprise. "You know about that?"

"Paige turned down an invitation to come to my house tonight just because you would be there."

Wes let out a breath before running a hand over his face. Nothing was ever as simple as he wanted it to be. "She didn't have to do that."

"She didn't want you to feel awkward."

"I just don't want her to get caught up in the middle of all this." How had everything become so messy? One day, he felt on top of the world. The next, everything seemed to be falling apart.

"You also canceled on her for helping with the Lantern Beach Scrub a Dub Dub."

Cassidy knew that as well? Of course she did. "It's not like that. The more Paige is around me, the more of a target she is. I just want her to be safe. I'm trying to do the right thing."

"Why don't you just tell her this instead of beating around the bush? Wouldn't that make things simpler?"

"Wait—did you talk to Ty?" That had been his exact advice also.

She raised an eyebrow. "Ty knows?"

Wes sighed. "That doesn't matter."

Cassidy leveled her gaze. "You should just tell her."

"Oh, come on." He raised his hands in the air, more emphatically than he'd intended. "You want me to tell Paige I have a stalker? What kind of man says something like that?"

"One who has a stalker." Cassidy's expression remained deadpan.

"Real men don't have stalkers. We're protectors, not victims."

She studied his face. "You really like her, don't you?"

Wes shrugged, suddenly feeling hot. This was not the conversation he wanted—or anticipated—having tonight. "I do like her."

Cassidy knocked her fist into his shoulder. "Then don't let things end like this. I expected more from you."

His jaw flexed. Cassidy just didn't understand this situation. "I'm trying to look out for her."

"That's not how it seems. It looks like you're being a jerk."

He flinched as her statement slapped him in the

face. "You really have a way with words, don't you, Cassidy?"

"Someone has to say it. Might as well be me." She put her notepad away and gave him a knowing look. "I'll write up this report, and we'll keep our eyes open for this woman. Do you have a picture?"

"No, but I can send you a link to her social media."

"That will work. I also need her name, age, contact information, and any other pertinent details." Cassidy took a step back toward her police cruiser. "And Wes, if she's as crazy as you think she is, be careful. We don't need any more drama here on this island."

"I agree with that. I don't like drama either."

"Keep your eyes open. I'll keep my eyes open also."

"Will do."

As Cassidy left, Wes glanced across the water at the sunset. It really was a beautiful one tonight. People on his tour would have gone crazy over it.

He wanted nothing more than to share the sight with Paige. What was he going to do? Come clean? Or attempt everything within his power to stay far away—for her sake, not his?

CHAPTER FIVE

THE NEXT MORNING, Wes headed to a plumbing emergency . . . at the RV park where Paige was staying. Though it had only been less than forty-eight hours since they'd spoken, Wes had to admit that he missed her company.

After he'd cleaned up his site last night and called the insurance company, he'd gone to Ty and Cassidy's to hang out with his friends for a little while. But he hadn't been able to stop thinking about Paige. About how she should have been there.

What had she ended up doing last night? Did she hate him for not calling?

His muscles tensed as he pulled down the gravel street, early morning sunlight washing over the area. He wished he didn't have to be here right now. That he didn't have to risk running into Paige. But the rec hall at the campground had a waterline backup, and he was the only plumber on the island. Normally, that was a good thing. Today, not so much.

He slowed his truck when he saw the silver Airstream with a small deck out front, complete with two cozy lounge chairs. He and Paige had sat on those chairs many times, talking about their lives. Their dreams. Their futures.

Not their future together. They hadn't been that serious. But he'd hoped that one day they might be.

Wes's stomach still clenched when he remembered everything that had happened. Even though he was no longer with Jennifer, she was still ruining things for him. Going out with her had been one of his worst choices ever.

As he spotted Paige's car beside her camper, he hit the brakes. He parked his truck and hopped out. Walking to the other side of his vehicle, he peered at the windshield.

It had been smashed.

His heart pounded in his ears as he saw the cracks spiderwebbing through the glass. Who had done this?

A door squeaked open, and Paige sauntered onto the deck.

He sucked in a breath when he saw her. She wore beige linen pants and an olive-colored tank top. Her curly hair fell around her shoulder in crazy ringlets, and her big eyes were full of surprise.

Her gaze went from Wes to her windshield then back to Wes. "What . . . ?"

"You didn't know about the window?" Wes pointed to her car.

"No, I had no idea." Her hands went to her hips, and she stared at him quizzically. "Not to be blunt, but why are you here?"

He couldn't blame her for her cold response. He deserved it after going radio silent on her.

"I'm doing a job down the road. I happened to be driving past when I saw it." He did a doubletake as her expression darkened. The truth hit him. "You don't think I did this, do you?"

She stepped down closer to him, a frown pulling at her lips. "I don't know what to say. I walked out to see you here, and the window was smashed. I guess . . . I don't know. I just thought . . ."

"Why would I do this, Paige?" He tapped his chest to emphasize his words.

"I have no idea. Then again, I don't really know you, do I?" Her voice trailed with hurt as she stared at him. The words hadn't been biting. No, they were filled with hurt.

Her eyes showed betrayal, showed a wall that was going up to protect herself from any future hurt.

Maybe Wes deserved it. If only Paige knew he'd put distance between them for her own good. Would she ever understand that?

He raised his hands. "I was just trying to help. You didn't hear anything?"

"No. Then again, Marky Mark over there has been blaring music since five a.m." She nodded across the street to a junky RV with speakers on a makeshift deck. "It's no wonder I had no idea. I had to put earplugs in just so I could sleep."

Any other time, Wes might smile at her description. Not today, though. "What about the people on either side of you? Could they have seen anything?"

"No one is occupying those RVs right now." She tilted her head. "You look overly concerned. Why? I feel like I'm missing something here."

He swallowed hard, trying to find his words. "It looks like someone did this purposefully, Paige. I'm surprised you're not *more* concerned."

"Honestly, I work for the police department. We see vandalism all the time. It was probably some bored kids or some thugs who got drunk and decided to cause some trouble. I've seen worse."

He stepped back and nodded, realizing he'd outstayed his welcome—if that's even what you'd call it. His plan to put distance between the two of them hadn't gone over well. "Okay then. I just want you to be careful."

"I appreciate your concern. But I'm careful. Thank you."

She was definitely unhappy, and Wes understood that. But he didn't want to do anything that might give the impression he cared about her—just in case Jennifer was watching. This was going to be one of the hardest things he'd ever done, though.

"By the way, thanks for the flowers," Paige muttered, apology in her gaze. "Sorry I didn't call to let you know I got them. I've been feeling slightly guilty about that."

He froze, hardly able to breath. "The flowers?"

Paige's eyes narrowed as she shrugged. "The daisies? I assumed you sent them. Should I be embarrassed right now?"

All the blood disappeared from his face so quickly that he felt dizzy. "Someone sent you daisies?"

"Okay . . . I guess that wasn't you. My mistake." She took a step back, looking ready to run. "It looks like I have another secret admirer."

Wes hardly heard her.

Had Jennifer done this? She was the only one who fit.

His gaze met Paige's as all his doubts disappeared. "We need to talk."

———

PAIGE STARED at Wes from the seat on her deck, unsure if she'd heard him right. Thankfully, she had the good sense to make some coffee before listening to what he had to say. She let the steam and soothing aroma of the drink hit her face as she composed her thoughts.

But only one realization remained at the forefront of her mind. She wanted her daddy now more than ever. Wanted him to tell her everything would be okay. Wanted him to wrap his arms around her in a bear hug. Wanted him to help her fix her car and advise her on how to handle things.

She drew in a shaky breath and cast those thoughts aside.

"Let me get this straight." She said the words slowly, desperate to know if she'd heard him correctly. "You think the person who sent me flowers and the person who smashed my window are one and the same."

Sweat sprinkled across Wes's face as he nodded. "That's correct."

"And do you know who this person is?" She seriously wondered if Wes was losing it right now. Not only was he not acting like himself, but his story didn't make much sense. Why would a secret admirer damage her car?

He let out a long breath and squeezed his eyes shut. "Look, I know how this is going to sound. I was hoping I was wrong, but I think that's less and less likely."

"Who do you think is responsible?" It was like Wes was putting off giving her an answer. Why in the world was he so nervous? Wes normally didn't get frazzled. He remained calm and cool, with a laid-back, self-deprecating kind of humor about him.

His hands went out in front of him, almost as if he grasped an imaginary object or tried to pull something solid out of thin air. "It's like this. I dated this girl when I lived in Virginia Beach who had a thing for daisies, and now I think she's here in town."

"Okay . . ." Paige still wasn't following. "You think your ex-girlfriend sent me flowers."

He shook his head a little too quickly. "It's more complicated than that. She's . . . she's not quite right."

"She's a scorned lover bent on revenge?"

He squeezed his eyes together. "It sounds weird when you say it like that."

"But is that what you're saying?"

He shrugged and opened his eyes. "In so many words, yes."

"I . . . don't know what to say. Why would she send me flowers *and* smash my window?"

"Because she's playing a troubling game and because she's vindictive."

"But you and I aren't even dating. Why would she target me?"

"She must have seen us together. I think she sees you as a threat."

Paige stared at him a moment, not saying anything, until asking, "Does Chief Chambers know about this?"

"I told her last night when holes mysteriously appeared in all of my kayaks."

She winced. "Oh, no. That's not good."

"It's not. My tours are postponed for the time being."

"Have you actually seen her?" Paige continued.

"I thought I saw her after we went paddleboarding, but she wasn't there when I checked. Half the time, I feel like I'm losing my mind."

"I can imagine."

He pulled his gaze back up to Paige. "That's why I have been trying to separate myself from you. I don't want her bothering you. The only way that's going to happen is if she doesn't perceive you as a threat."

"That explanation would have been nice earlier when you canceled our plans and stopped talking to me," she said in a soft, chiding voice.

"I know. I deserve that, and I deserve any other hard feelings you have toward me. I just don't want to see you get caught up in this."

She remembered her car windshield. "It sounds like it's too late."

Wes reached forward and touched her arm. A spark sizzled through her at his touch.

He seemed to feel it too as he pulled away and swallowed hard. "Keep your eyes open, okay? Be careful."

The breath left her lungs as she realized what he was saying. "You think she'd go as far as hurting me?"

"I have no idea, but I wouldn't put much past her. In the meantime, I can't talk to you in person for a while, Paige. Part of me wants to stay close so I can keep you safe. But I don't think it's going to work that way."

Though Paige was disappointed, she understood what he was saying. She didn't want this ex-girl-friend to come between her and Wes. But maybe with time all the drama would pass.

"I guess I should call the chief," she finally said.

Wes nodded somberly. "Yeah, I think you should. And Paige? I'm sorry. I'm really sorry."

Paige stared at him a moment, realizing she was sorry also . . . sorry that Wes's history along with her own seemed to be working against them.

CHAPTER SIX

THIS WASN'T the way Paige had wanted to spend her Tuesday. First, she'd seen Wes. Then she'd seen her smashed window. Then she'd heard Wes's story.

She still wasn't sure what to think about all he'd told her. He'd looked sincere and burdened, so much so that Paige actually felt bad for him. If he was telling the truth, then she could understand why this was difficult for him.

Unfortunately, in her experience, men weren't always honest. She wished she had some kind of internal lie detector that would clue her in. Instead, Paige had to trust her gut—which had failed her more than once before.

Her high school boyfriend Mikey had "acciden-tally" fallen in love with her best friend. Paige had lost both the guy she'd been in love with and her confidante in the same day. Then recently, there had been Owen and the devastating consequences of being with him. She'd chosen him over her family and in the process had made the biggest mistake of her life.

Now Paige felt all alone, and sometimes incapable of both trusting someone else and trusting herself.

All she wanted was to fall in love with someone who'd love her unconditionally, who'd offer her the kind of support she'd once had at home. She wanted the kind of love that erased all doubt.

Sometimes that felt like the most absurd fantasy of all.

Before coming to work, Paige had called Chief Chambers, who'd come out and filed a report. Once that was over, Paige had taken her car to the only garage in town.

Thankfully, the mechanic there had said he should be able to fix it today. The bad news was that it would cost three hundred for the new windshield. Her deductible was five hundred, so insurance wouldn't cover this.

Finally, Paige had gone to work, but she could hardly concentrate on the paperwork she was supposed to file. Instead, she kept looking through the glass doors at the front of the building for anyone who was acting strangely.

She'd seen no one.

"Hey, Paige." Chief Chambers emerged from her office and stopped near her desk. "Want to grab a late lunch at The Crazy Chefette?"

Her spirits lifted at the possibility. "I'd love to."

"Perfect. I'll drive."

A few minutes later, they were situated in the chief's SUV. They made chitchat as they drove down the road and pulled up to The Crazy Chefette. Once inside, they were seated at a corner booth with glasses of water. The savory smell of bacon mixed with the sweet scent of vanilla wafted around them.

The eatery carried menu items unique on the taste buds. Paige's favorite was the grilled cheese with peaches. She'd balked at the idea at first, but after she'd tried it—at Wes's urging—she'd loved it. The whole place was a real gem of a find here on the island.

Paige glanced around the dining area. Thankfully, she didn't see anyone suspicious.

Her shoulders relaxed some. Maybe she was making a big deal out of nothing.

Chief Chambers didn't even pick up her menu. Instead, she turned to Paige. "So, how are you holding up?"

Paige shrugged, considering how to answer, how much to say. "I've been better."

"So, Wes told you the whole story? I ran into him at the gas station earlier, and he told me you'd had a conversation."

"He sure did. I hardly know what to think." The whole explanation still seemed surreal, more like a Lifetime movie than real life.

The chief offered a compassionate frown. "Anyone in a situation like this would feel the same. What can I do for you?"

That was a great question, and she appreciated the chief's thoughtfulness. "I'm not really sure. I'm still trying to comprehend the fact that Wes's crazy ex-girlfriend could be on the island and targeting me."

"It's a lot to comprehend. We're all on the lookout for her. Did you see a picture of her so you'll recognize her?"

"Yes, Wes showed me before he left." The woman in the photo had looked normal—perky, happy, bright. But those weren't words Wes had used to describe her.

Chief Chambers laced her hands together in front of her and leaned closer. "If you don't mind me asking—and I realize this is none of my business— what did you two decide?"

"That we should stay away from each other." Paige's heart thudded as she said the words. She understood why Wes felt that way . . . it just seemed like such a shame.

"Maybe it's best until we figure out what's going on. I know he doesn't want you to get hurt."

"I suppose you're right, Chief." Paige ran her hand over the menu. Wes's whole story just seemed so unbelievable. And how things could go from great one day to avoiding each other at all costs the next still perplexed her. Then again, she was too loyal at times, so she erred in the opposite way.

"Listen, when we're not at the station, just call me Cassidy."

"It's a deal."

Cassidy leaned toward Paige. "So, we've been working together for a month or so, but we haven't had much time to talk. What really brought you to this area, Paige?"

She welcomed the change of subject, even though her past wasn't exactly pleasant. "To be honest, coming here wasn't really in my plans. Sometimes, you have to change with the current and see where it takes you. The current brought me here."

"You mentioned something about a boyfriend and Wilmington . . ." The chief stared at her from across the table, not looking like she was interrogating her but like they were two friends having lunch together.

Owen's image flashed in her mind. "My boyfriend got the 'opportunity of a lifetime' in Wilmington, so I moved from Florida to be near him until we got married. Unfortunately, marriage was never really in his plans. He was the type who was always looking for bigger and better fish in the sea. He liked the rush of hooking the latest catch."

"I'm sorry."

"Me too." Her dad had warned her that Owen was no good. That he'd be nothing but trouble. Her father should know—Owen had worked on her dad's boat before the man had gotten fired for stealing.

But Paige had thought her heart knew more, knew better than her father. She'd been wrong. So, so wrong.

Once Owen's true colors were revealed, Paige knew she couldn't stay in Wilmington. But she also knew she couldn't go home to Florida—not after the way she'd left things there. Her dad had been so angry when Paige had told him she loved Owen.

They'd been standing outside their house, the bay glimmering in the distance and the pier where she'd taken her first step stretching over the water.

Her dad's eyes had been lit with a passion she rarely saw. He'd told her if she chose Owen then she shouldn't ever come back. His words felt like a slap in the face.

Her mom had stood behind her dad with tears streaming down her face as she listened to it all. Owen had stood near the car, waiting for Paige's decision.

There was no compromise. Paige had to choose. Her family or Owen.

The memory still felt like a punch in the gut.

"Why Lantern Beach?" Cassidy asked, taking a sip of her water. "Besides the current bringing you here."

Paige shrugged. "I guess I've always loved island life. My dad was a fisherman. He'd spend four months at a time out on the water. It wasn't a life full of means and money. But it was a good life, growing up by the sea down in Florida."

Paige drew in a shaky breath. Cassidy said nothing, just waited for her to continue. Paige tried to hold her emotions at bay until she could finish.

"Anyway, I've always known I wanted to live in a small, coastal community like my hometown," she finally said. "One of the ladies from my church in Wilmington told me about Lantern Beach and how great it was. I initially came just to visit, but I quickly fell in love—with the town," Paige quickly added.

Cassidy flashed a smile. "It sounds like it. We're certainly glad to have you here."

The chief's smile faded as her phone rang. She took the call using her professional voice. When she ended the conversation, she glanced at Paige with a frown.

"I'd really wanted to talk more," the chief said. "But there was a car accident out on the highway. I'm going to need to head out there so I can take statements. As you know, our other guys are tied up with a domestic dispute at the moment."

"I'll be fine here."

She twisted her head. "You want me to call you a ride?"

"No, it's not that far from the station. I can walk if I have to." Besides, the weather was nice today. Some fresh air might feel invigorating.

The chief nodded and rose, dropping a couple dollars on the table first. "Okay, if you're sure. I'd love to chat again sometime, if you're up for it."

"I'd love to." It had been nice to have a female to visit with, to open up to. Cassidy always seemed wise beyond her years, like she'd be the perfect big sister.

With the chief gone, Paige glanced around the restaurant. Tourists clustered at most of the tables. She could spot them because of their new beach clothes and sunburns. The town doctor—Clemson—sat at the bar area talking to Mac MacArthur, the former police chief and current mayor. A younger woman who operated the island's only ice cream truck stood near them, and she reminded Paige of an anime character with her stark makeup and boldly colored clothes.

Lantern Beach.

Paige hoped to make a fresh start here. She knew it would take time to make friends and establish herself. But she truly could see herself becoming part of this community.

Then she'd met Wes, and she'd realized everything she'd been missing when she dated Owen. Owen had initially been charming—but none of it had been real. He was the type who used people to get what he wanted.

Wes, on the other hand, wasn't the type who cared about impressing people, and that had been so appealing. He paved his own way, giving up his career to move here to this island and live the life he wanted.

Paige shook her head, pushing those thoughts aside. Wes might seem perfect, but that didn't mean he was for her. Sometimes it took a variety of circumstances to see a person's true colors. That had been the case with Owen, and it had been the case with the man she'd dated before him.

She was a poor judge of character when her heart was involved. She'd be wise to keep that in mind and not make the same mistakes.

"Good afternoon!" someone said beside her.

Paige looked up and saw Lisa Dillinger standing there. She owned this restaurant—she was the original Crazy Chefette herself. Paige had instantly liked Lisa, with her big smile and bubbly personality. Lisa was organizing the efforts to feed volunteers after the Scrub a Dub Dub event on Friday.

"Good afternoon." Paige tucked a curl behind her ear and smiled.

"You're here alone?" Lisa glanced at the empty seat in the booth across from Paige.

Yes, she and Wes had quickly become a pair here on Lantern Beach. But now that was over . . . wasn't it? She was still confused about what all of this meant for their relationship.

"It's just me," Paige finally said. "Cassidy had to run. I thought I'd grab some lunch while I wait for my car to get fixed."

"I see. Well, take your time with the menu. I'll be right back to take your order. We're a little short-staffed today, so I'm pulling double duty. I apologize, but Angie, my new waitress, fell asleep at the beach and got sun poisoning."

"Ouch."

"Yes, ouch. And her blisters aren't the most appetizing thing to look at when you're ordering food. Anyway, I'll be back in a minute."

"Sounds good. Thank you, Lisa."

Paige stared down at the menu, knowing she'd probably order her favorite meal. But she thought she'd give the other selections consideration, just to be fair. After all, the Jalapeño Popper Soup sounded pretty good also, as did the Burger with Butter— peanut butter, that was.

"Excuse me," someone said.

Paige looked up, fully expecting to see Lisa standing there again.

Instead, a woman with dark hair and glasses paused beside her booth. She looked vaguely familiar.

"Yes?"

"I need to talk to you." The woman slid into the booth across from her, a deep frown creasing the sides of her mouth. "It's about Wes."

CHAPTER SEVEN

PAIGE EYED the woman in front of her, wondering if she'd seen her before. Wondering how the stranger had found her here. This wasn't Jennifer—she didn't look like the picture. But could she be another scorned girlfriend?

Or *was* she Jennifer? Paige stared at the woman, trying to see beyond the hair color and glasses. She supposed the two women might look similar, but Paige had only quickly seen Jennifer's picture.

She glanced around. They were surrounded by people. Whoever this woman was, Paige should be safe enough talking to her out in public like this.

She'd hear what she had to say—for a few minutes, at least.

"What about Wes?" Paige's voice sounded strained as she asked the question. She was guarded, and she would remain so until she had more information.

The woman stared her straight in the eye, unflinching. "I'll just get right to the point. I heard he has his sights set on you."

"His sights set on me?" That was a strange way to word it. "I don't know about that. Who are you?"

She pressed her neatly manicured hands into the table, displaying a nice-sized engagement and wedding ring. "I know Wes. We go way back. And I felt the need to warn you about him."

"Did you . . . track him down here?"

"No! I'm on vacation with my husband, and I just happened to see Wes."

Her explanation could be plausible. But Paige needed to hear more. "Why would you warn me about him?"

Something about this conversation already made Paige very uncomfortable. First, the fact that the woman had found her. But the vague answers also left her unsettled.

"He's a player, to start with." The woman lowered her voice and leaned closer. "He burned me once, and I wished I'd listened to the warning someone had given me. I didn't, but I don't want to see someone else make that same mistake."

"You don't have to worry about that. Wes and I . . . well, there *is* no Wes and I."

There never really had been, and this morning had seemed to seal the deal, so to speak.

A strange emotion passed through the woman's eyes. "There isn't? You could have fooled me."

Paige jerked her gaze up and nearly stuttered, "You've . . . you've been watching us?"

The woman's eyes widened. "No! I told you, I didn't expect to see Wes. But I happened to stumble across the two of you on the beach one day. That's all."

Paige pressed her lips together. Was this woman telling the truth? The explanation sounded logical enough. Either way . . .

"It doesn't matter. Wes . . . isn't ready for a relationship." Paige didn't owe this woman any more of an explanation than that.

The woman nodded and offered a slight shrug. "Okay then. I guess this warning was for nothing."

Paige studied the woman another minute. She seemed sincere. But Paige still couldn't let down her guard.

"I know Wes can seem like a real catch. That's what makes this situation so difficult."

Paige remembered all the fun they'd had together.

Was that all a sham? She didn't know. But she wasn't ready to completely buy this woman's story yet.

"Yes, he can be charming," Paige said, deciding to play along for a little while. "What exactly is your story?"

Before the woman could answer, Lisa appeared at their booth. She smiled at Paige before looking curiously at the woman across from her. "Welcome to The Crazy Chefette. Would you like a menu?"

"Oh, no. I'm not staying." She waved her hand.

"Please do stay." Paige was interested in hearing more of what this woman had to say. She knew Wes, had a history with him, and Paige wanted to know more.

The woman twisted her lips as she stared across the table, looking uncertain. "Are you sure? I'd hate to impose."

"Yes, I'd like some company. Unless your husband is waiting for you . . ."

"He's actually on a fishing tour right now." The woman nodded slowly, thoughtfully, and finally leaned back. "Okay then. I'll stay. But I don't need a menu. I'll just have whatever she's having."

"I'll have my usual," Paige told Lisa.

"Very well then. Grilled cheese with peaches, a personal favorite of mine also." Lisa turned with a playful flourish. "I shall return."

As Lisa left, Paige turned back to the woman across from her. "So, back to my question. What's your story with Wes?"

The woman shrugged and leaned back, her gaze scanning the restaurant. "We dated. I thought we were going to get married, but apparently he had no intention of that. He just wanted a good time."

Paige flinched. She didn't want to view Wes like that. All he'd been was respectful to her. Sure, he may have broken her heart a little when he'd ghosted her, but he hadn't been a world-class jerk.

But people had types, didn't they? And whether or not Paige wanted to admit it, the type she chose also had been unreliable. Untrustworthy. Liars.

She squeezed her eyes shut. She desperately didn't want Wes to fit that pattern. Yet, part of her wouldn't be surprised. It was like she had a radar for men who cheated.

"I know what you're thinking. Could this be the same Wes? Believe me—it is. He started off sweet and kind and concerned." Her expression darkened. "But he changed."

"I'm sorry to hear that." Men who acted like one person to win a woman's affection and then trans-formed were the worst types. Paige had prided herself on being careful, but, in the end, she hadn't been immune to men like that after all.

"Yeah, me too." The woman rubbed her arms, as if chilled. "It got bad toward the end."

"What do you mean by bad?" Paige was honestly curious now. Had Wes just been a player? Or was there more to this story?

Her stormy gaze met Paige's. "I mean, he actually broke my car window when I tried to tell him to leave me alone."

"What?" Paige's voice climbed in pitch. That didn't fit the image she knew of Wes. Besides, Ty and Cassidy trusted him. That said a lot about his character. Still, she kept listening.

"I know, it's crazy, right? He started off so normal. But there's a psycho hiding down deep inside him." She shivered again.

"He smashed your car window?" Paige repeated, certain she hadn't heard correctly. She'd wanted to give Wes the benefit of the doubt this morning but . . .

"Why do you say it like that? Wait . . . did he do the same thing to you?"

This morning's events flashed back to her. "My windshield was smashed. Wes was the one who happened to drive past and discover it. I thought it seemed like too much of a coincidence." That had been her gut reaction, but she'd ignored it. Was that a mistake?

"I'm telling you, it's all a game to him. He covers it up really well, though."

Paige's stomach twisted. She didn't want to believe that was the truth. She wanted to believe that Wes was the fun-loving guy she'd met. That he was a hard worker with a wicked sense of humor and tender eyes.

But her dad had always told her if something seemed too good to be true, it probably was. It looked like her father was right again.

"By the way, I never caught your name. Mine's Paige." She studied the woman another moment, waiting for her response.

The woman smiled. "You can call me Jen."

CHAPTER EIGHT

PAIGE STOOD as the realization hit her, her knee smacking the table and rocking water over the top of her wobbling glass.

This woman *was* Jennifer. Wes hadn't told her the woman was now married. True, he may not have known or the woman could have been lying. Still, at the same time, Paige felt like she'd been tricked.

Wes had made the woman sound like poison. Was that what this woman was doing? Planting destructive seeds in her mind? Or had she been speaking the truth?

"I know about you," Paige murmured. "*You're* the one who smashed my windshield."

Jennifer's expression hardened as she raised her chin. "That's what Wes told you, isn't it? You only heard half the story."

Paige shook her head, not willing to believe anything else Jen said. "I don't need to hear anymore. The fact that you're here on this island speaks for itself."

"Like I said, I came here for vacation with my husband. I never expected to see Wes. And, when I did, I almost left. I didn't want him to see me. Then I saw he had someone else in his snare, and I changed my mind. I knew I had to warn you. It was my duty, woman to woman."

"I don't believe you." Paige started to take a step away. She didn't need to hear anything else. Wes was *not* the bad guy here.

"He's not the person he claims to be," Jennifer said.

"He's a good person." Despite their history, she'd seen Wes in action. He'd selflessly acted to help save his best friend's life when Ty had been abducted. He'd filled in for Lisa and helped her deliver meals to the homebound here on the island. He even helped a stray dog find a new home.

He wasn't a psychopath.

Jen let out a snort, as if Paige had just told an unbelievable joke. "I wasn't going to tell you every-thing. I was hoping the CliffsNotes version could do the trick. But you need to stay away from Wes. I'm telling you this for your own good."

"Why?" Paige leaned closer, not one to be easily scared off. "Are you going to hurt me if I don't?"

Jen stared at her a minute before shaking her head. Her shoulders softened and a somberness washed over her. "Is that what he told you? That *I* was the crazy one?"

Her words caught Paige's attention. What did she mean by that?

Paige said nothing, only waited. She didn't want to know, yet she did.

Jen pulled out her phone, hit a few buttons, and then showed Paige the screen. "This is what happens when things don't go according to Wes's plan."

Paige gasped when she saw the picture there.

It was Jen. With blonde hair, just like in her social media photos.

But gone was her smiling face. Instead, one eye was bruised. Her lip was cut. Her gaze was lined with fear and grief.

"What are you saying?" Paige asked, her voice now trembling. "That he did this to you?"

"That's exactly what I'm saying. I tried to break up with him, and this is what happened. He told everyone that I was the crazy one. That I'd done it to myself. A lot of people even believed him. It still makes me sick to my stomach to think about." Tears filled her gaze.

Paige shook her head and sat back down, determined to hear more and figure out the truth. "I can't believe Wes would do this to you. He would never hurt a woman."

Jen wiped her eyes with a napkin from the table. "That's what he wants people to believe. But it's not true. You can try to convince yourself it is. But you're just going to end up being the victim in the end."

Paige leaned back, still reeling from the conversation. "Thanks for your concern, but . . . I can't take things like this at face value. Those are some pretty big accusations."

"Then maybe you'll believe this." She pulled up another photo on her phone and showed it to Paige.

Paige glanced at the screen. It was a police report. For Wes.

He'd been arrested for assault and battery.

Paige's stomach sank. No, that couldn't be. But she'd seen the evidence with her own eyes . . .

What if Jen was right? What if all of this, everything that had happened, was just a ploy by Wes to manipulate her?

She swallowed hard as nausea churned in her stomach.

Had Wes lied to her? Not only that, but had he beaten another woman and then tried to paint her in a bad light?

If that was the case, Paige had to figure out what to do.

Because she could be dealing with someone dangerous here.

———

WES HAD SPENT the day working various plumbing jobs and remaining alert for any sign of Jennifer.

He hadn't seen her.

But every time he thought about Paige's windshield, both a shiver of fear and a bolt of anger seemed to move parallel inside him.

He had to find Jennifer if he was going to put an end to this craziness. He wanted to locate her, make sure she was taken into custody for the vandalism of his kayaks and Paige's car, and then he wanted to move forward. With Paige. To tell her how he really felt. To explore the possibility of a real relationship further.

He never thought he'd feel like this again. But he did. He liked Paige. He really liked her.

After working, he'd gone back to his place and began the task of patching his kayaks. It would take some time, but he hoped to have them operational again by this weekend. He'd already canceled tonight and tomorrow night's excursions.

He couldn't afford to cancel much more or his business would be a wash, costing more to operate than it brought in. It had never been a big money maker—instead it had always been a labor of love. He truly enjoyed showing people the beauty of Lantern Beach from a different perspective while out on the water.

Finally, after working on six kayaks, he decided to take a break for the evening. He didn't mind working hard, but there also needed to be time to relax and have fun. Otherwise, he should have stuck with his nose-to-the-grindstone job in advertising.

He changed into some shorts and a T-shirt and grabbed his keys. As he climbed into his truck, Paige's image filled his mind. He'd love nothing more than to go to her place and talk. To really talk. To explain things.

But he resisted, reminding himself that she was safer without him near. There would be time for that in the future—he hoped.

Instead, he headed over to Ty and Cassidy's for a game of sand volleyball.

He liked to squeeze in hanging out with his friends whenever he could. Several of them had met at a Bible study at church, and the group had grown from there.

Of course, now almost everyone in the gang was married or paired off.

Ty and Cassidy had their whirlwind romance.

Austin and Skye had finally declared their feelings for each other after years of being best friends.

Lisa and Braden had discovered they were perfect together.

Even Pastor Jack, who was a late addition to the group, had found love after losing his first wife.

Wes was now the odd man out.

That was okay. Wes didn't mind standing alone.

At least, he hadn't until he met Paige. Somehow, she'd changed everything for him. She'd made him wonder what life would be like with someone by his side.

He'd held out for only the best. He'd wanted someone he could have fun with. Have an intelligent conversation with. Someone who made him laugh. Who had a good work ethic when needed and knew how to kick back at other times.

Paige had been all of those things.

He sighed. There was no use thinking about it now.

He drove across the island to the other end, where Ty and Cassidy's home was. He pulled into the driveway and then climbed the dune.

His friends played volleyball on the other side as

the ocean waves crashed behind them. Not everyone was here. Their work schedules hadn't allowed that. But there was a good two-on-two game going on that he wanted to join. It would be good to burn off some stress.

"Hey, Wes," Ty called from his position as referee. "Glad you could make it."

"Of course." He pulled off his shirt and walked toward the sand volleyball court. "I'm ready to win some games."

"One more serve, and you're in," Austin said, holding the ball next to his hip.

He stood on the sidelines, watching the game and thanking God for such a good group of friends. As he did, Lisa walked up to him, a sweaty glass of lemonade in hand.

"Hey, you!" she started. "I saw Paige today."

He swallowed back a moment of regret at how things had transpired between him and Paige. "Is that right? Did she come into The Crazy Chefette?"

"She did. A friend met her there."

His muscles tightened as an ominous feeling stirred in his gut. "A friend?"

"Yeah, this woman with dark hair and glasses. They seemed to get along really well."

Wes froze. Dark hair and glasses? That didn't

sound like Jennifer—unless she'd changed her look. Still, something didn't sit right with him.

"But it was weird," Lisa continued. "I brought their food, but they were both gone. They left some money on the table for me, of course. Something must have come up. It got me a little worried, though."

"Did you catch her friend's name?"

"No, I didn't. Why?" Lisa frowned. "Is something wrong?"

Wes pulled his shirt back on. "I need to find Paige."

"Did I say something?" Lisa asked, looking confused.

"No, but I've got to go. Tell everyone I'm sorry."

CHAPTER NINE

PAIGE FELT SLEEP TRYING to claim her as she lounged on the couch in her RV after work. She wanted to get outside. Wanted to enjoy the weather. Maybe go kayaking or do something to keep her mind occupied with subjects other than her conversation with Jen.

But her muscles weren't cooperating, and all she wanted to do was remain on her couch in a nearly comatose state.

She hardly ever felt like this. She was Ms. Outdoors. Ms. Energetic. Ms. Active.

But not right now.

Maybe the emotional struggle of the past couple months was catching up with her. Or she was coming down with a virus. That was the only thing that made sense.

Most likely, it was that conversation with Jennifer. Every time she thought of those photos, she felt the life drain from her.

She couldn't have made those things up, right? They'd looked real. Jennifer had looked sincere. She'd cried even.

Paige closed her eyes, tired of fighting how sleepy she felt. Maybe she should just rest. Maybe her body was trying to tell her that's what she needed.

Before she could drift off to a restful place, a loud knock sounded at the door.

She flinched. Who in the world was here? Maybe she would ignore the sound. Sleep seemed so much better than getting up.

"Paige, it's me. Wes. Open up."

Her eyes flung open. Wes. Was he here to convince her he was innocent in all this to manipulate her into believing him? She might have fallen for that before. But not again.

"Go away," she yelled, willing her voice to sound louder, tougher. But she didn't have the energy to make it happen.

"I need to talk to you. Please."

"I don't want to talk." There was nothing he could say. Paige had seen the proof of his actions with her own eyes. She'd never be able to forget.

"Paige, please. I need for you to hear me out. I think you could be in danger."

"From you?" Cynicism edged her words.

He paused for a minute before saying, "What?"

She wanted to tell him to go away again. But maybe she would confront him about his lies. Otherwise, he would keep doing what he was doing and hurting more people.

She remembered the picture Jen had shown her with her face bruised and swollen.

No woman should have to go through that.

And that was exactly what Paige was going to tell Wes, even if there were consequences.

She dragged herself off her couch. Her limbs felt heavy as she lumbered toward the door and threw it open.

As soon as the fresh air wafted inside, a second wind returned to her. Her head suddenly seemed clearer. Her thoughts less fuzzy.

Holding onto the doorway to steady herself, Paige stepped outside into the darkening evening and took another deep breath. She tried to form her thoughts, but they were still blurry. Her lips weren't cooperating.

"Are you okay, Paige?" Wes touched her arm, a concerned look on his face.

She flinched and pulled away a little too hard. She

nearly fell back into the RV. What was going on with her? Something felt off.

"I'm fine." Her words slurred.

Wes's eyes narrowed "You don't look fine."

"I was just resting." That was it. Paige was tired. Wes had pulled her from her slumber. No other explanation was needed.

He glanced behind her before taking her arm. "Have a seat on the deck for a minute."

"Are you trying to boss me around?" Her words slurred again.

"Please, Paige. Just listen to me."

She didn't have the strength to argue. He led her to the chair, and she nearly collapsed there. Her head spun as she sat on the wooden slats.

Once she was secure, Wes walked around the outside of the camper. She had no idea what he was doing, but worry kicked in. Something was wrong with her, but she had no idea what.

Wes returned with a grim look on his face and the phone to his ear.

"What is it?" she asked.

Wes had found something, hadn't he? She couldn't imagine what.

Wes said a few more things before putting his phone away and turning back to her. "Someone connected a hose to the exhaust of the RV next door, the one you said was unoccupied. They ran the hose into the window of your RV and left the engine going."

"But that would give me . . ."

"Carbon monoxide poisoning. Yes." He took her arm and tugged her to her feet. "I need to get you to the clinic."

"I'll be fine—" She just needed some fresh air.

"Please, don't argue. We need to have you checked out."

"But—"

"Paige, please."

The earnest sound of his voice stopped her arguments in their tracks. Paige nodded. Maybe she should be checked out. Because she didn't feel like herself right now.

And she needed to feel like herself if she was going to confront Wes about his lies.

———

WES SAT OUTSIDE of Paige's room at the clinic as Doc Clemson examined her. When they'd arrived here, she'd had her blood drawn. Then she'd been given an oxygen mask and would need to stay on O_2 for several hours to get the carbon monoxide out of her bloodstream.

Three hours had already passed.

Meanwhile, Cassidy had gone to Paige's RV to check out the hose and question Paige's neighbors. Wes was waiting to hear what she'd learned—and hoping that Cassidy would share anything pertinent.

But Wes already knew the truth.

He knew that Jennifer was in town, just as he'd suspected. That she was the one who'd run that hose from an RV into Paige's. If he hadn't gotten there when he did . . . he didn't even want to think about it. Just as before, Jennifer was escalating—and that thought terrified him.

Doc Clemson stepped out of Paige's room a few minutes later. The man was in his sixties with ruddy skin, yellowish orange hair, and a twisted sense of humor. He also worked as the island's medical examiner.

"She's going to be fine," Clemson said. "You found her in the nick of time. That's the good news. But she will need another hour or so on the oxygen. She can take a little break, if need be. You're welcome to see her . . . if she's okay with it, of course."

"I'm not!" Paige called from the other side of the door.

Wes resisted a smile. Paige was feisty. That must mean she was feeling more like herself.

But his grin dimmed as he remembered the

conversation they needed to have. Jennifer must have filled her head with lies. Why else would Paige be so abrasive right now?

"I'll leave you two to work things out." Clemson raised his eyebrows. "Let me know if you need anything—except a mediator. That's not in my job description."

"Got it."

Wes's heart turned heavy again as he knocked at her door. He knew this conversation wouldn't be pleasant. But it was necessary.

He pushed the door open. He'd back off if Paige told him to—but he needed to see her face first, needed to know she was sincere. More than anything, he wanted to clear the air, and he prayed she didn't turn him away.

"I know you're not very happy with me right now, but could you spare a few minutes for the man who may have saved your life?" Wes asked.

She said nothing for a minute before crossing one arm and taking her oxygen mask off with the other. "How do I know you're not responsible for my attempted demise? That you didn't set yourself up to be the hero?"

Her words felt like a slap in the face. He'd expected many retorts, but not that one. "Why would I do that?"

"I don't know. As a matter of control?"

"Paige . . ." Wes stepped inside, his voice pleading with her for understanding.

His heart lurched when he saw her in the hospital bed, though. Her hospital gown . . . the pale skin . . . the oxygen mask . . .

The sight reminded him of just how close that had been. There could be very different results right now if Wes hadn't arrived when he did, and he thanked God she was still alive.

"How are you feeling?" He paused by her bed, waiting for her to send him away.

He hadn't kissed her yet. But as he stared at her now, he had the strong desire to pull her into his arms and show her how much he cared.

He resisted.

There was romantic. And then there was creepy.

If he did kiss her now, it might fall into the creepy category—especially considering the tension between them.

Paige narrowed her eyes, her voice cracking as she said, "Please tell me you didn't do this."

"You think I ran an exhaust line into your RV? Why would I do that?" Was this one of the effects of the gas? Delusions? Why in the world would she even think that?

"Like I said, so you could be my savior. So I'd run

to you for protection. I don't want to believe it, but . . ."

"And again I ask, why would I do that?" His voice climbed with frustration. She wasn't making sense. Or maybe he just didn't want to put the pieces together.

Paige's narrowed eyes became even smaller. "I know about you, Wes. I know how you operate. I only regret I didn't know that sooner."

He ran a hand over his face, feeling like he was fighting a losing battle. "We need to talk, Paige. You talked to Jennifer today, didn't you? Lisa said she saw you at the restaurant with a woman she didn't recognize."

"I did. You made her out to be a monster, and she was anything but. Now you're going to try to convince me that you're noble, that you're the victim, and then you'll proceed to treat me like trash also."

Wes felt the blood drain from his face. That was exactly what he'd hoped he wouldn't hear. Lies. More lies.

But now he knew the stakes were higher than ever.

He had to set the record straight—now.

CHAPTER TEN

PAIGE WATCHED as Wes's face lost its color—just as she expected it might. He'd been discovered, and now he was going to try to make excuses to explain his actions.

She'd seen it before. He'd do his best to make Jennifer look like the bad guy. Yet part of her hoped she was wrong. That all this was wrong. That Jennifer *especially* was wrong.

Wes lowered himself into a chair at her bedside, his usual playfulness gone and replaced with edginess. "What did Jennifer tell you exactly?"

Paige remembered her conversation with the woman. But first, she put the mask over her face and breathed deeply, giving herself a moment to get her thoughts together. "She told me that you liked to play games."

"What kind of games?"

"Painful ones." She leveled her gaze with Wes, deciding to cut to the truth. "I saw her photo, the one of her after you beat her. I saw the police report too. I know you were charged."

Wes sucked in a quick breath before swinging his head back and forth. "I did *not* do that to her. Those charges were dropped. That's what Jennifer told you? That I did that to her?"

Paige stared at his face. At the tight lines. She remembered the defensiveness in his tone. Were those things signs of guilt? Or was he speaking the truth after someone had verbally slandered him?

If it was the second scenario, Paige could understand. She'd want to defend herself also.

"Yes, that's what she said." Paige inhaled deeply. "She said you were violent."

"And you believed her?" His voice rose with surprise. Was that hurt in his gaze? His expression made her momentarily regret her words. But Paige had to ask these questions. She'd be a fool if she didn't.

"Why wouldn't I believe her? I saw the evidence with my own eyes. I only regret I didn't see it sooner." Paige had been such a fool. She was just thankful she'd seen the light before she got in too deeply.

"You really think I would do those things, Paige?" Wes leaned closer, staring into her eyes.

His green eyes tried to mesmerize her—but she couldn't let them. He might look sincere, but that didn't mean he wasn't just a great actor.

But Paige had to ask herself: Did she really think Wes would do those things? She didn't want to believe it. But the evidence was to the contrary.

She licked her lips. "You discovered my broken windshield. You discovered the exhaust pouring into my RV. I'm thinking that everything fits so far. Your manipulation is at expert level. It would be impressive if it wasn't so sick."

"Paige, you know me better than that."

"Actually, I don't. I don't really know you, Wes. We've had fun together. We've talked about generic things. We've goofed off. But I really don't know that much about you at all. I don't know what shaped you into the man you are today. Why you really came here to Lantern Beach. I don't know your biggest regrets or your fears or what makes you cry."

"I would love to go deeper with you, Paige."

Paige said nothing. She appreciated his words, but were they too little too late? She had to figure that out.

Wes reached for her arm but stopped short of actually touching her. Instead, he dropped his hand back down to the side. "Paige, please don't believe anything Jennifer told you. She wants nothing more than to ruin me, and to ruin any of my future relationships."

She studied his gaze. "Why shouldn't I?"

"Because she's crazy."

"She told me you'd say that." Paige would need more than that if he really wanted to convince her he was the victim here. Words . . . they could be empty. They could be easy. What she needed was the truth.

"Paige, I need you to listen to me. She's not stable. You need to stay away from her."

His excuses were disappointing . . . he offered no new information, only vague warnings. "Wes, I'm not sure I want to hear your cautions. It sounds to me like you're trying to deflect your issues on someone else. It's a typical pattern for abusers."

He ran a hand over his face, his eyes squeezed shut. Finally, he opened them again and stared at her. "Paige, please. Just give me five minutes to explain things. Five minutes. If you still don't believe me . . . then I'll walk away. I promise. Please. You'll never have to see me again."

She saw the earnestness in his eyes and finally nodded. "Fine. Five minutes. But not a minute more."

———

WES SUCKED IN A DEEP BREATH, grateful that Paige hadn't kicked him out. But she still could.

Where did he even start? Would Paige believe him? He had to give it a shot, at least.

"After I'd broken things off with Jennifer, she showed up at my house one night," Wes started. "She begged to get back together. I told her no. She asked to come inside. I said no, that we'd never be together again."

Paige didn't say anything. She just listened, pulling the oxygen mask back over her face and waiting for him to continue.

"The next morning, the police showed up at my house and arrested me. They told me that Jennifer had come into the station covered in bruises. She'd told them I was responsible for them."

"And?" Paige asked beneath her mask.

"And . . . it just so happened that I was recording a video presentation with one of my coworkers that evening. My story could be verified due to the time stamp on the recordings. It showed that I'd left the computer for five minutes—not nearly long enough to do the damage Jennifer said I'd done."

"Keep going."

"The police checked my hands. There were no

bruises. They talked to the neighbors. No one saw anything. They talked to my coworker. He verified that I didn't seem out of breath or like I'd been in a fight. The charges were dropped."

"Then how did she get the bruises?" Paige asked, her expression softening some.

"That's a question for Jennifer. My theory is that she did it to herself. She's that sick and twisted."

Paige studied his face a moment before putting her oxygen mask aside and narrowing her eyes. "You told me about your relationship with her. Why would you keep that detail from me? It makes it seem like you're hiding something."

Wes dipped his head, hating the fact he had to defend himself from accusations that had no basis in reality. "I didn't tell you because none of it was true. It was a lie. What would it prove if I had mentioned those charges? It would only make you doubt me."

"It makes you look . . . violent."

Injustice churned inside him, causing a surge of passion to rise in his voice. "Exactly. Once accusations like that are thrown out—even if they're not true—they're almost impossible to bounce back from."

Paige studied his face again. "Is that really why you moved here?"

"I really moved here to get away from all of that

craziness. And . . . I didn't like working in advertising. Truth is, I like being a blue-collar worker. I've been on both sides of the career spectrum. Work borne with sweat and muscle is still important. It doesn't make someone any less of a person, despite what some sides of society might preach."

Paige smiled for the first time, but it quickly disappeared. "I agree. Tell me more. How did you two meet each other?"

Was she feeling him out for holes in his story? Probably.

He let out a breath. "Like I said, I met Jennifer back when I lived in Virginia Beach. Things started out great between us but quickly went south. She wasn't the girl I thought she was. I started noticing little things about her. She'd check my email for me. She found the spare key to my house and let herself in. That she went out of her way to get to know my friends."

"Maybe she was trying to make a good impression." Even Paige's voice held doubt.

"Maybe. I gave her the benefit of doubt at first also. But it quickly proved that I should have listened to my gut. It went from bad to worse."

"What happened?"

"Everything escalated. She let herself into my apartment whenever she wanted. She answered my emails for me—even to my work colleagues. I saw the writing on the wall. I broke things off. I did so nicely and kindly. But she didn't take no for an answer."

"What does that mean exactly?"

"I started dating someone else a couple weeks later—nothing serious. Jennifer kept showing up wherever this new girl went and spreading lies about me. She said she and I were still dating. Every time I tried to date someone, Jennifer pulled stunts like that."

"That's . . . rough."

"I think she broke your car window and pulled the stunt today at your RV. And it's no mistake that she's trying to befriend you. She wants to get into your head." Just the thought of it caused anger to course through his veins. But it was one thing to feel anger, and an entirely different story to act on it.

Paige shook her head, exhaustion beginning to wear on her features. "How do I know that you're not the one who's messing with me?"

"I guess you don't, Paige." Wes shook his head wearily. "But I'm concerned for your safety. I thought if I separated myself from you, she'd leave you alone. I can see that's not the case. I don't know what to do now. How can I keep you safe if I leave you alone?"

"I didn't ask you to keep me safe, Wes."

"If something happens to you, it's going to be my fault."

Paige rubbed the skin at her temples and closed her eyes. "I don't even know what to say. I need . . . I need a moment to think this through."

"I'm going to wait outside."

She nodded resolutely. "I'd expect nothing less."

"I'm worried about you, Paige." Wes meant the words. He was concerned. Jennifer was taking this to an entirely new level.

"I just need some time. It's a lot to process."

He lowered his voice. "I know it is. But I'll be outside in the hall if you need me."

He really hoped—and prayed—that she didn't push him away.

CHAPTER ELEVEN

TWO HOURS LATER, the doctor cleared Paige to leave. The problem was that Wes had driven her here to the clinic, and it was the middle of the night.

She glanced at the time. Three a.m. to be exact.

Who else would she call to take her home? Cassidy? Did she even want to go back to her RV after what had happened there?

She sighed and splashed some cold water in her face. She'd slipped into the bathroom to freshen up before departing. She grabbed some paper towels and dabbed her face, glancing in the mirror as she did so. Paige cringed. Even she had to admit that she looked tired—both physically and mentally.

She knew one thing. She wanted to trust Wes. She wanted to believe his story. He'd sounded earnest.

Her problem was that Jennifer had also sounded earnest.

So which of them was telling the truth?

Her mind raced through the possibilities. The truth was Wes had one big thing on his side: his friends. Paige didn't really think that Ty, Cassidy, and the rest of the gang would be buddies with someone like the person Jennifer described.

Or had Wes fooled them also? Was he the type who could charm anyone but devastate the ones who meant the most to him?

Paige didn't want to believe that. But she needed to be wise here.

When she exited the bathroom, she asked the nurse to send Wes into the room. He stepped inside, exhaustion evident on his features. The sparkle was gone from his eyes, and the sight of that caused her heart to lurch.

This had been hard on him too, hadn't it? What if he was innocent? If that was the case, he was just as much a victim here as she was.

"So, I guess you're cleared to leave," he started, jamming his hands into his pockets.

"That's what I heard." She ran a hand over her shirt, pressing out imaginary wrinkles.

"Do you want me to see if Cassidy can pick you up?"

Paige shrugged, appreciating the fact that he wasn't being pushy. Though she still had her reservations, too many people knew she and Wes were together right now for him to do anything stupid—if he was even guilty of doing any of those things. He'd be a fool to make any wrong moves now.

"Actually, I'd be grateful if you would assist in that," she finally said.

A spark of hope lit in his eyes. "I'd be happy to."

"But no flirting with me." She wasn't trying to flirt, but her words had sounded more playful than she intended.

"I would never dream of it." A flicker of a smile curled his lip before disappearing.

"I mean it."

He cocked his head to the side. "What are you going to do if I do flirt?"

"I'll write up a police report myself. Assault with awful one-liners."

He chuckled and bobbed his head up and down. "I'll keep that in mind."

He led her out to his truck, and they climbed inside. He cranked the engine and let it run for a minute. The AC filled the cab, and Paige leaned her face into it.

"Where would you like to go?" he asked.

That was the question Paige had been asking

herself. She just couldn't bear the thought of going to her RV.

"I . . . don't know," she admitted.

He paused. "Look, I have an extra room at my house. You're welcome to stay there. Otherwise, I can call Cassidy and—"

"Your place would be great." Had Paige really just said that? She had. She realized there was no other place she'd feel safer . . . and she craved the familiar. But those feelings clashed with her uncertainties, leaving her head throbbing.

Should she take her words back?

Wes glanced at her, as if unsure he'd heard correctly. "You sure?"

Was she? Wes would never hurt her. But was that what Jennifer had believed also?

She swallowed hard as a solution came to mind. "Yes. But I'll be sleeping with a knife. I need to make that clear."

He opened his mouth as if to argue and then shook his head, halfway humored. "Whatever works for you."

———

PAIGE'S THROAT felt tight as she stepped into Wes's cottage. She'd been here before many times, so she shouldn't feel awkward. But it was nearly four a.m., and their relationship already seemed to have a long history—and the two of them weren't even dating.

His place was simple, with wood-paneled walls and outdated kitchen cabinets. But it was clean. His couch was brown leather. The pictures on his walls displayed lighthouses from up and down the East Coast.

If this was her place, Paige would paint the paneling to brighten up the space. Add updated frames to the photos. Add some colorful pillows to the couch.

"You can stay in the spare bedroom. No one ever uses it, so it should be good to go."

She forced a smile. "Thank you."

As she stared at him standing there, she wanted nothing more than to experience one of his hugs. She wanted comfort and assurance and to know she wasn't all alone in this crazy world. She wanted a human touch—Wes's touch.

But that was a bad idea. The smartest thing she could do was to keep her distance.

She cleared her throat. "Listen, do you mind if I grab some water before I head to bed?"

"Of course. I'll get it for you. Do you want an orange slice?"

She smiled. Wes remembered her preference. She

loved a little citrus in her water. "Only if it's no trouble."

As Wes disappeared into the kitchen, she paced to the couch and sat on the edge. She wished she was tired. She should be tired. But instead, adrenaline pulsed through her. It was going to be hard to find sleep tonight, unfortunately.

Wes handed her an icy cool glass and then sat down a comfortable distance from her on the other end of the couch. She took a long sip.

"Are you okay?" Wes asked. "I mean, are you really okay? I know this has to have shaken you up."

"I'm . . . I'm okay. I think."

"I know you're probably uncertain about whether or not you can trust me. I just want to say that I would never raise a hand to a woman. Never. I'm sorry if Jennifer has muddled your thoughts."

Jennifer had definitely muddled her thoughts. Paige's heart clashed with the reality of what she'd seen—those pictures. The police report.

What should she believe? She didn't want to be stupid.

"In the morning, call the Virginia Beach Police Department. Maybe Cassidy can help you cut through any red tape. If you ask them, they'll tell you that those charges were proven false."

She took another sip of her water. "Maybe I'll do that."

If Wes told the truth, he was living out his own *Fatal Attraction*.

And if Jennifer had really gone through all this trouble to make Wes look like the bad guy . . . then there really was something wrong with her. Majorly wrong.

Paige shivered.

Where was Jennifer right now? Was she watching them? Had she watched them . . . leave the clinic? Come here?

Another shiver wracked Paige's body.

What kind of person would do something like this? Running that exhaust line could have been fatal for Paige.

As much as her doubts plagued her, deep in her heart, she couldn't see Wes doing something like that. But what if she was wrong . . . again?

She cleared her throat. "I think I will go to bed. Thanks for letting me stay here."

"Of course." He rose and pointed behind him. "You want to grab a knife first?"

That's right. Paige had said she was sleeping with a knife. She let out a soft chuckle. "No, I think I'll be okay."

"Good to hear." Wes slowly walked her down the hall to the room.

Tension stretched between them as they stood face-to-face by her door. That invisible cord was always there, always seeming to draw them together.

Under different circumstances, they might hug goodnight. Not a short hug either. A long, lingering one. She might kiss his cheek. She might dream about what it would be like to do more. To kiss his lips.

Instead, Paige pushed a hair behind her ear and croaked out, "Goodnight, Wes."

His eyes practically seared into her soul as he looked down at her. "Goodnight, Paige."

She slipped into her room before she lost all her resolve.

Jennifer's plan would either work to pull them apart and develop distrust between the two of them . . . or it would totally backfire and pull them closer together than ever.

Paige's heart was rooting for the latter.

CHAPTER TWELVE

PAIGE HAD HARDLY SLEPT last night. Every time she closed her eyes, nightmares haunted her. Nightmares about her conversation with Jennifer. About dying in her sleep. About Wes sneaking into her room and finishing her off.

By the time she climbed out of bed, it was eight a.m., and she felt like a zombie.

She had to be at work in an hour. Since she had no clothes here, she'd have to face her RV again and get herself cleaned up.

In the meantime, she glanced in the mirror and nearly flinched at her reflection. She did her best to smooth her curls before she stepped out of her room. The aroma of bacon sizzling filled the air, making her stomach grumble.

She paced toward the kitchen and paused, watching

Wes as he stood at the kitchen counter. He fried some bacon with one hand and tried to flip a pancake with the other. She smiled, instantly wanting to help him, yet enjoying the moment too much to move.

Could this man really have a violent side? She hated that she kept having to ask herself that question, but she needed to be smart.

And Paige just couldn't see it.

Yet, she needed to remain cautious. She'd never thought Owen was capable of the things he'd done either.

Her smile dimmed at the thought.

Wes glanced back just then and spotted her. "Good morning."

She shook off her concerns and stepped forward. "Morning. You've been busy."

"I thought some food might help both of us feel a little better today. I don't know about you, but I hardly slept a wink last night. Too much on my mind."

"Same here." She joined him at the counter and took the spatula from him. "Let me help with these pancakes."

He flashed a quick grin. "Thank you."

The food was done a few minutes later, and they sat at the table in his kitchen. Paige was suddenly starving and couldn't wait to dig into the pancakes and bacon.

"Cassidy called," Wes started, taking a sip of his orange juice. "She wanted to check on you."

"That was sweet. Any updates?"

"No, not yet. They talked to all your neighbors, but no one saw anything. Last I heard, they weren't able to find any usable prints on the hose running to your RV. They're also looking all over the island for Jennifer. So far, they haven't found her."

Her stomach sank. She'd been hoping for better news. "That's too bad."

Wes nodded. "I was hoping for more also. Cassidy also said you need to take today off work."

Paige raised her eyebrows as she picked up a piece of her bacon. "I don't know about that. I have a lot to do, especially with the Beach Scrub a Dub Dub coming up—"

"She thought of that and said you could do it from home."

"Home?" Her throat burned as she said the words. She didn't really want to go back there. But she would if she had to.

"Or from here," Wes added with a slight shrug. "You're welcome to work on the event from here."

She tried to read his expression. Did that mean he

wanted her to stay here? That he felt better with her close by? Or was the gesture flippant?

"You need to go into work today also, don't you?" Paige finally said. "I don't want to keep you from—"

"I took the day off."

"You don't have to do that."

"I only had one job, and it wasn't an emergency. Someone wants me to change a sink fixture for them. No big deal."

"And you plan on babysitting me instead?" She watched his expression.

"Babysitting?" He narrowed his eyes, like the idea was absurd. "I would never word it that way. This is what I do know. It's my fault you're in this mess. If anything happens to you, I won't forgive myself. That's the most important thing to me right now—keeping you safe."

"I'm flattered . . . I guess."

"I'm not trying to flatter you. I just can't stand the thought of you being hurt on my account." His words rang in the air.

Paige felt her cheeks flush. She quickly turned back to her food, desperate for something to distract her. "I appreciate your concern."

"Your wish is my command. Let me know what you need, and I'm here for you."

"That's sweet of you." She ate her last bite of

bacon and pushed her plate away, trying to think everything through. Sitting around all day with nothing to do sounded like a recipe for disaster.

"What do you want to do?" Wes asked.

What *did* she want to do? Go back to the RV? No, that sounded awful. But what else could she tell him?

She closed her eyes a minute, and her mind went to her happy place. The place that always calmed her down.

"I want to doublecheck a few things for the cleanup event—it should only take less than an hour," she said. "And then I want to go out on the water."

"Out on the water?" Wes stared at her and waited for more of an explanation.

"That's right. Kayaking. Paddleboarding. Windsurfing. I'd even go out in a rowboat. I just want to feel the wind on my face and going through my hair."

He raised his cup of coffee and nodded slowly, thoughtfully. "Okay then. I can make that happen."

———

AN HOUR LATER, Wes and Paige were on a catamaran, sailing over the waters of the Pamlico Sound. They'd briefly stopped by Paige's RV so she could get her swimsuit and change. She'd seemed nervous to go back inside, but she'd done it anyway. Wes had waited just outside her door, on guard for any signs of trouble.

There had been none.

The day was perfect for enjoying the water, and being out here was the ideal way to recover from yesterday's events. Besides, out here there was no one but him and Paige. If trouble was coming, they should be able to see it a mile away.

He glanced at the other side of the boat where Paige sat. The wind blew her hair away from her face, revealing sun-kissed cheeks and friendly freckles. She looked like she belonged out here on the water.

They'd had many conversations before, but none of them had gone very deep. If he asked personal questions, he'd been afraid Paige might ask personal questions as well. So they'd keep things light. They'd talked about dream vacations and favorite hobbies and the best ice cream flavors.

Suddenly, he didn't really care anymore. He wanted to know more about Paige. About what made her tick. About why she really came here.

Because Wes might have secrets—he couldn't deny that. But Paige also had a few of her own.

"You really love the water, don't you?" Wes started.

"What can I say? Water makes me feel like I'm at home."

"But you left your home in Florida . . ." Why had she left if she loved it so much?

She shrugged and stared out over the horizon. "I did. Initially it was for college and a job. I mean, it was a small town. There weren't many jobs there unless I wanted to fish myself, which I didn't. My dad always said it was never the job for a lady. I figured a lady could do the job just as well as a man—I just didn't want to."

"So you got a job somewhere else after college? With Fish and Wildlife, you said?"

She nodded and pulled the tiller toward her to turn away from the wind. "I did. I think everyone always thought I'd come back. But I needed to know I could stand on my own two feet first."

"Why?"

She let out a breath. "My best friend and my high school boyfriend fell in love with each other—accidentally, they said. In a strange way, I was happy for them while still being heartbroken for myself. We lived in a small town, and I kept running into them."

"That sounds terrible."

"It was. It's hard to explain, but I just knew I .

needed to get away, to prove that I could survive—and thrive—without my best friend. Without a boyfriend. Without my parents paying my bills."

"I thought you said before that your ex-boyfriend was older?"

She frowned. "I've only dated two men. Mikey and Owen. Owen is four years older than I am. I met him when I came home to visit my parents."

"What happened with him?"

"Owen worked for my dad. He seemed perfect—he was fun, the life of the party, a hard worker. Then my dad caught him stealing some money from him. That's what my dad thought, at least. Owen insisted that he'd been set up, that my dad just didn't like him and wanted a reason of get rid of him."

"Did that seem like your dad?"

"No, not at all. But Owen was very convincing. The way he explained everything made perfect sense. And I was so in love with him that I didn't see clearly." Tears filled her gaze but she seemed to quickly pull them back. "In the end, I had to choose between my family or Owen."

"I see." That would explain the sad look she sometimes got in her eyes.

"Foolishly, I believed Owen. I told my dad that he'd gotten things wrong, that Owen wasn't like that. Dad argued with me, and things escalated. I told my dad I couldn't believe he would sink so low as to frame Owen, just to get rid of him." A tear trickled down her cheek.

Wes didn't say anything. He just listened.

"I followed Owen up to Wilmington. He'd promised that we would get married and build a life together, and I was so in love that I believed him. Then one day . . . I caught Owen with another woman, and I realized it had all been lies. All of it. My dad was right . . . but it was too late to undo the choices I'd made."

"Is it ever truly too late?"

She wiped the moisture beneath her eyes. "Unfortunately, yes. It's . . . complicated. I knew I didn't want to stay in Wilmington, but I couldn't go home either. So here I am." She looked at him. "How about you? How did you get here?"

Any lightheartedness Wes had felt disappeared, but he didn't mind talking about his past anymore. He needed to put the truth out there. "I wanted a fresh start also . . . away from Jennifer."

Paige's smile slipped. "I see."

"Honestly, though, up in Virginia Beach, I was working for an advertising firm. My dad had been a plumber, and he taught me the trade. But he wanted a better life for me. Insisted I go to college. I just kind of stumbled into the marketing and advertising world. My best friend was studying it, so I figured, why not? Nothing else really interested me. After college, I got a job, and I did well for myself. But my heart was never really in it. I like working with my hands. Being outdoors. Moving."

"Those things fit you."

"After Jennifer . . . everything kind of came to a head, and I knew I had to make a choice. She wasn't going to let me have a life in Virginia Beach. So I quit my job, packed a few things, and came down here. I didn't tell anyone but my family where I was going. And I decided to do what I loved. I didn't care if I made a lot of money or not. I just wanted enough to live on."

"It takes courage to take those steps."

"Listen, I know you're still probably uncertain about Jennifer." Wes's voice dipped. "I'm sorry about that. I really am. I've kept my distance from women for a long time out of fear that Jennifer would somehow find out. She's not right, Paige."

"She just seemed so nice . . ."

"I know. That's what makes her even more dangerous." As he said the words, he looked out in the distance. A boat was coming their way.

Certainly the driver would see their colorful sail and veer away from them.

But he'd seen too many moments where those

behind the wheel had been drinking too much or weren't paying attention. It was just as dangerous in a boat as it was in a car.

"What is that guy doing?" Paige muttered, her eyes fixated in the distance.

Wes's muscles tensed. The boat should have turned by now.

He pushed the tiller away from him to straighten the rudder and move out of the boat's path.

But the boat changed course.

It headed right toward them.

Wes knew with certainty that wasn't a coincidence.

CHAPTER THIRTEEN

PAIGE STARED at the boat as it sped toward them. Alarm raced through her. Fear froze her muscles.

The boat was going to hit them any minute. There was no way they could sail away quickly enough to beat it.

One look at Wes's face, and she knew he felt the same way.

The boat's motor roared closer and closer.

Paige waved at the driver, trying to get his attention. To get him to turn. To correct his path.

But whoever was behind that wheel wasn't paying attention. A floppy hat and oversized sunglasses covered his face, not allowing them to see where he was looking.

Or where *she* was looking.

The thought caused the color to drain from her face.

Could this be Jennifer?

Paige couldn't get a good enough look at the driver to tell.

"Paige," Wes called.

She pulled her gaze away from the boat long enough to say, "Yes?"

"When I count to three, we've got to jump."

"We're so far from shore right now." Land was only a sliver in the distance.

"We have no choice. You can do this." Wes glanced at the boat. "One."

Paige braced herself for what was about to happen. She had a life jacket on. But she knew they were far enough out that the current would determine where they ended up—and it could be the ocean if the water pulled them far enough toward the south.

"Two."

The boat was only a few feet away. She tried to see the identification number on the side, but it was coming at them too fast.

"Three!" Wes grabbed her hand, and they dove into the water. They surfaced in time to see their catamaran split into uncountable pieces.

Paige's heart raced when she saw the wreckage.

That could have been her and Wes.

The boat sped away, unaffected by the collision.

As Paige floated there, she stared at the driver one more time.

She couldn't tell if it was a man or a woman. If it was Jennifer or not.

But, for the time being, she was just thankful to be alive.

Now she and Wes had to figure out a way to ensure they stayed alive.

———

"ARE YOU OKAY?" Wes studied Paige for any sign of injury as they treaded water. Other parts of the sound were shallow, but they were far enough out that the water was easily over their heads. Paige's hair clung to her skin and shock was evident on her face. In the distance, he heard the buzz of the boat as it sped away.

Paige swallowed hard. "I'm fine. You?"

"Ticked off, but otherwise okay." He glanced in the distance. "We're a good mile and a half from shore. We're going to have to work against the current here."

"I know."

He swam toward the wreckage and grabbed a

piece of the hull. "Let's hold on to this. It will keep us together and help keep us afloat."

"I was thinking the same thing." She swam over and held on.

It was going to be a grueling swim back. But they had no other choice. Wes had brought a radio with him, but his things were scattered everywhere now. He didn't see his waterproof box.

"Come on," he said. "Let's do this. We'll take our time and move at a steady pace. We don't have to go fast."

Together, they kicked their legs and began moving toward the shore. If they even stopped for a moment, the current and wind were going to send them back out—and they couldn't let that happen. But with persistence, they would make it back to shallow water and then they could walk the rest of the way to the beach.

He just needed to keep Paige calm. Keeping her talking. Distracted.

He knew these waters like the back of his hand. Thankfully, both he and Paige were fit enough to pull this off.

"Do you think that was Jennifer?" Paige asked, sounding slightly breathless as she clung to the wreckage.

"It's my best guess." He felt his expression darken as he thought about it.

"Why would she do that? She could have killed us."

"Because she thinks I belong to her." Even saying the words aloud left him with a sick feeling in his stomach.

Paige frowned but gripped the wreckage tightly, her tanned bicep flexing and showing her athletic physique. The determination in her eyes let him know she would get through this.

"That sounds like a bad made-for-TV movie," Paige said.

"Believe me, I know. It's not something I go around telling my friends about." He knew this was no time to let his pride get in the way, not when people's safety was on the line. But he'd really hoped to bury this part of his past.

Paige glanced at him, studying his face a moment. "So you really haven't been serious with anyone since her?"

"I went out with a few women after Jennifer. That didn't go well. When I saw how Jennifer went after anyone I showed interest in, I knew I was done."

Paige was the first person he'd met in a long time that made him want to reconsider his position.

But now that was proving to be a mistake also. His interest in her might get her killed.

"How are you doing over there?" Wes glanced at Paige out of the corner of his eye.

"I'm fine. My dad used to call me a fish. I practically grew up in the water."

Her dad . . . maybe this would be the perfect opportunity to get to know her more, beyond the superficial. "When did you talk to your dad last?"

Her lips pulled down in a frown and somberness washed over her. "It's been three months. He doesn't want to talk to me."

"Are you sure about that?" Her words had sounded so final, so sad. He knew for certain there was more to this story.

"I'm pretty certain."

"Well, I, for one, am glad you came here to Lantern Beach." He kicked harder, fighting the current and the wind around them.

A smile flickered across her face. "Thanks, Wes."

Maybe there was hope that Jennifer hadn't totally ruined things between them.

Maybe.

CHAPTER FOURTEEN

FINALLY, Paige felt the sand beneath her feet. They were still a good way out from the shore, probably a quarter mile, but the water here was shallow. They could let go of their piece of broken boat and walk the rest of the way in. That was good. Because she was tired.

If she'd been with any other swimmer than Wes, they might not have made it out of that current. It had worked hard against them.

Paige still shivered when she thought about how close they'd come to dying . . . again.

Maybe she shouldn't be hanging out with Wes. Yet she loved being around him.

She hated the uncertainty she felt after her conversation with Jennifer. The woman could be lying . . . but what if she was telling the truth?

Yet, when Paige had talked to Wes today while they were sailing, he'd seemed nothing but sincere.

Her decision might be easier if she hadn't made such bad judgment calls in the past.

Like with Owen. He'd fed her lie after lie about working late. In actuality, he'd go out fishing and return earlier than what he'd told her. Paige happened to run into him at a restaurant with another woman. He'd been holding her hand and staring deeply into her eyes.

That's when all the lies became clear.

In fact, Owen had most likely done the same thing to Paige down in Florida. She just hadn't put the pieces together until that day at the restaurant when she'd seen it with her own eyes.

Suddenly, Wes let out a yelp beside her.

She glanced over as he pulled his right foot from the water. Blood dripped from his sole.

"Wes, are you okay?" The cut looked deep.

He grimaced but said, "Yeah, I'm fine. There must be a broken bottle down there."

She stripped her shirt off. She had a bathing suit on beneath it, unlike Wes—who wore only a life jacket and shorts right now. "Here, tie this around it."

He leaned against her for balance as he wrapped the shirt around his foot and tied it in place. That would help until they could clean it.

She slipped an arm around his waist and helped him the rest of the way back. As soon as they reached dry sand, they both collapsed there, lying on their backs and staring at the sky. That had been close. Too close.

"We need to call that in," Paige murmured.

"Yes, we do." He drew in several more deep breaths before sitting up with a moan. "I'll call from the truck. I don't think we need to stay here for any reason. The boat . . . it's long gone and there's no evidence here on this shore."

"Good point," Paige said, water dripping from her clothes and her skin tightening under the heat of the sun. "Where are your keys? I'll drive."

"You want to drive Frisco?"

She flopped her head toward him, sand sticking to her damp curls and skin. "You named your truck?"

"Doesn't everyone?"

"No. It's a little strange."

"Why? Naming boats isn't strange. What so different about trucks?"

"You're strange." A smile tugged at her lip.

He poked her arm with his index finger. "Oh, I see how you are."

She raised an eyebrow, hating the way her body reacted to his touch. Even something as simple as a playful poke got her blood pumping. "No flirting, remember?"

"This isn't flirting. This is banter."

She pushed up on her elbows, knowing she needed to get control of the situation. "We should go clean your wound."

"You're probably right." He stood and followed after her.

Paige tried not to let on, but she was so grateful to be on dry land.

Yet she knew this wasn't over yet. How would it end? With Jennifer being arrested? Or with Paige being dead?

———

WES TRIED NOT to show how thrilled he was to feel Paige's arm around him as he hobbled inside his cottage. To feel her springy curls brushing his skin.

Once inside, she led him to the bathroom, turned the water on in the tub, and then ordered him to sit down and put his foot in the water. He did as he was told.

"Where's your first aid kit?" she asked.

"Below the sink."

She dug around and finally pulled it out. She began shuffling through it until she found what she was looking for. In the meantime, the water hit his cut. He tried not to flinch.

"Are you sure you don't want to go to the clinic?" Paige pulled out a bandage.

"I'm sure. And, before you ask, I'm up to date on my tetanus shot." This was just a cut. He didn't need stitches or anything.

She scowled and continued to rifle through supplies, looking for what she needed. "You made me go after the incident at the RV."

"That was different."

She paused long enough to put her hand on her hip and level her gaze. "Why? Because I'm a girl?"

"I didn't say that."

"You didn't have to." Paige threw him a light-hearted look before grabbing some antiseptic.

"I had to make sure the exhaust hadn't messed with your head."

She cocked an eyebrow. "You're saying something is wrong with me in the head?"

He chuckled and ran a hand over his face. "I just can't say anything right, can I?"

She sat on the edge of the tub beside him, still looking playfully bossy. "Here, let me see your foot."

He moved it until she could rest it on her leg.

"This looks deep." She squinted as she studied it.

"It should be fine."

Carefully, she dried it and applied some ointment before putting a bandage over the wound. Wes watched her as she worked. She was so beautiful, so unassuming. Most people would be a mess after what she went through today. Not Paige.

He was never going to get this woman out of his system, was he?

The truth was, he didn't want to.

"You're pretty good at that." Wes swallowed the burn in his throat.

"I did work as a first mate on a charter fishing boat when I was in high school."

"Did you?" He raised his eyebrows. "I'm learning all kinds of new things about you."

"Aren't you, though?" She lowered his foot to the floor. "Now, can I please use this bathroom to clean up? I feel gross. Besides, I don't really want to go back to the RV. Not yet."

He stood, realizing he would do anything for Paige—anything to see her smile, to make her happy. "Absolutely. The towels are in the drawer. Take your time."

He left, closing the door behind him and trying not to wince as he put weight on his foot.

He felt such a mix of emotions. Joy from being around Paige. Trepidation at the thought of Jennifer.

He needed to figure out some resolution because they couldn't keep living like this.

He stepped into his bedroom, ready to get cleaned up himself. But, as he did, he froze.

What was that smell?

It wasn't typical of his bedroom. It was fruity. Almost like a perfume.

And that's when it hit him.

It was Jennifer's perfume.

She'd been in here.

What had she been doing?

CHAPTER FIFTEEN

PAIGE FROZE when she stepped out of the steamy bathroom and saw Wes standing at the end of the hallway. He hadn't changed clothes, but he did have a new expression on his face—a pensive look.

Instantly, Paige tensed. Something was wrong, wasn't it?

He met her halfway down the hallway. "Cassidy is here."

"Chief Chambers?" Alarm raced through her, and she touched her wet curls.

"She's talked to the marine police and such, but she'd like to take your statement while I get cleaned up."

There was something more to this—something bad. "What's going on, Wes?"

He stepped closer, that deep frown still on his

face as he lowered his voice. "I think Jennifer has been in here. I smelled her perfume in my room. I wanted someone to be on guard out here, just in case."

Just in case Jennifer came back, Paige realized with a shudder. This nightmare never ended, did it?

"Okay. Of course." Paige nodded, trying to appear more even-keeled than she felt right now. What she wanted to do was sink down on the couch with a warm blanket and pretend none of this was happening.

Wes brushed past her, headed back toward his room. As he did, she had the strange urge to reach up and touch his face. Try to somehow make him feel better.

Paige knew he blamed himself for all of this. He thought it was somehow his fault that Jennifer was doing these things.

But it wasn't. She had no idea how to make him believe that, though.

Instead, she walked into the living room and nodded at her boss. "Cassidy."

"Hey, Paige." Cassidy sat in a chair—not looking relaxed, like this was a casual visit. No, she perched on the end, looking all business.

Paige lowered herself onto the couch, wishing she'd brought more than her jean shorts and T-shirt.

At least she was clean now. "I guess Wes told you what happened?"

"Yes, he did. The situation is getting worse and worse."

"I know."

Cassidy studied Paige, a concerned expression on her face. "I want to hear your version of what happened with the boat."

Paige launched into her story, sharing all the details. As she finished, she frowned and glanced down the hallway to where Wes had disappeared.

"I've just never seen Wes like this." Cassidy sounded dead serious. "He's really worried."

"I can tell." His expression had said it all.

Cassidy's gaze caught hers, and suddenly she wasn't the police chief. She was Wes's friend. Paige's friend. A mix of protector and counselor. "He cares about you, you know."

Paige's cheeks flushed as her words rang through the air. "I'm the last person he needs to have feelings for."

"Why's that?" Cassidy tilted her head.

Sadness pressed on her as she mentally reviewed the facts. "Lots of reasons, starting with the fact that I don't even know how long I'll be here. I have terrible judgment when it comes to men. And . . . then there's everything Jennifer told me."

"What did she say?"

Paige told her, and Cassidy frowned with each new detail. "Wes would never do those things."

"You didn't see the pictures . . ."

Cassidy patted her hand. "I'm sure she was going for the shock value. But you'll figure it all out. You're smart."

"Maybe." Or maybe Paige should leave. Get out of here. Cut her losses before her heart was broken again or before she broke someone else's heart. But where would she go? Not home.

Would she find a new place to start again? The thought caused her heart to ache. She wasn't meant to be a nomad. She wanted more than anything to put down roots.

"Listen, it's not my business, but you told me at The Crazy Chefette that you came here because it was where the current brought you, right?"

Paige nodded, wondering where she was going with this.

"This is just something for you to think about. Sometimes, the most rewarding thing we can do is to go against the current. It's challenging. It's hard. But you can make your own way . . . and sometimes that's exactly what we need to do."

As the thoughts pounded her, the door to Wes's room opened, and he stepped into the hallway. Just the sight of him caused her heart to flutter out of control. His T-shirt showed his defined chest, his shorts showed muscular legs. But those weren't the things that really attracted her to him. It was his eyes —eyes that showed his heart.

They didn't lie, did they?

Cassidy stood and nodded briefly to Wes, then Paige. "I think I've got everything I need. I've got guys out there now looking for this boat. I hope we find it soon. In the meantime, keep your eyes open and call me if you need me."

"Will do, Chief," Wes said.

Paige watched as Cassidy departed. The tension of being alone with Wes returned. If Paige was smart, she would go. She'd give herself more time to sort out her feelings. To figure out what was true and what wasn't.

Instead, she fought the urge to touch him again. To pour her life into his. To forget her fears.

Something unseen told her to stay, to give Wes a chance.

She hoped she didn't regret it.

———

WES MOVED CLOSER TO PAIGE.

As Cassidy departed, she'd stood to say goodbye.

The two of them were in front of each other now, and Wes struggled to know what to say.

He'd heard the last part of Paige and Cassidy's conversation. Heard Paige and Cassidy talking about him. Whether or not Paige could trust him. He saw the doubt still present in Paige's eyes.

The pressure inside him felt like it might crush his heart.

He knew better than anyone that people's histories—their pasts—defined and shaped their views of future relationships. Those things had certainly shaped him. But still . . . he had to have hope that things could be better. That the past wasn't destined to repeat itself. That better things awaited.

Right?

He wasn't generally one to avoid conflict—not when it involved something he cared about. And he was very much starting to care about Paige.

"Listen, Paige," he started, pressing his lips together. "I know you still have doubts about me. I don't blame you. What Jennifer showed you was probably convincing."

"It was."

"Have I made mistakes in my past relationships? Yes, I have. There are things I'd change if I could do it all over again. I think we'd all say that."

Paige didn't argue.

"But I'd never purposefully hurt someone. I'm not a player. If I went out with a woman and knew after a couple dates we weren't going to work, I didn't pursue it. Nor would I ever raise my hand to a woman."

"Thank you for saying that." Paige stepped closer, a playfulness returning to her gaze. "You care what I think, don't you?"

"Is that bad?"

"Only if you're flirting with me."

He let out a laugh and stepped closer. "That's good to know."

"Isn't it, though?"

He started to reach for her waist but dropped his arms. If he touched her, he might forget everything he wanted to say, *needed* to say. "I'm not going to lie. I like you, Paige. That thought terrifies me."

"It scares me too." She licked her lips as she stared up at him.

"The fact that I like you?"

A smile cracked her face, and she shrugged playfully. "Well, yes. Partly. But the thought of falling for someone. There's just so much I don't know right now . . ."

Wes decided to stop hesitating. He reached forward. His finger slipped into the belt loop of her jean shorts, and he tugged her closer. Paige let out a laugh that sounded half nervous, half giddy. But her eyes turned serious as her gaze locked with his.

"You're definitely flirting," she murmured.

"Yes, I am." Wes leaned toward her, imagining what her lips would feel like against his. He couldn't wait to find out.

But before he could properly kiss her, something crashed through the window.

CHAPTER SIXTEEN

PAIGE JERKED BACK, clinging to Wes's arm as she tried to comprehend what had just happened. All she'd heard was a crash and glass breaking.

She glanced at the floor near her feet and saw a brick there.

"Stay here," Wes said, a steely determination in his voice.

He charged toward the door.

"Wes!" Paige reached for him. As much as she wanted Wes to figure out what was happening, she didn't want him to get hurt. Jennifer, assuming she was behind these attacks, was clearly a threat right now and seemed to be coming more unhinged by the moment.

Wes didn't seem to hear Paige—or he ignored her. He darted outside.

Tires squealed in the distance. Whoever had thrown that brick had taken off. They wouldn't catch her now.

Her.

Because Paige now felt sure Jennifer was behind this. But how were they going to prove it? And how were they going to stop her?

She had no idea.

Wes walked back inside, adrenaline pulsating from him. He was mad, and rightfully so.

He stormed over to the brick and pulled off a piece of paper that had been wrapped around it.

In crudely written letters, Paige read the message over his shoulder.

YOU'RE **mine and only mine. Forever. Nothing can separate us.**

A CHILL RACED up Paige's spine.

This wasn't going to end, was it? She knew it wouldn't. Not until someone was either seriously hurt or dead—and those somebodies could only be Wes, Paige, or Jennifer.

———

CASSIDY SHOWED up at Wes's house fifteen minutes later. Wes was used to seeing her on a friendly basis. But having her over so often to investigate? He didn't like it.

Nor did he like the extreme measures Jennifer was going through to get his attention.

He didn't know how to keep Paige safe. Or even worse—he didn't know *if* he could keep Paige safe. That answer wasn't acceptable.

The three of them stood in his living room, hot air seeping in through the broken window beside them and Wes's irritation growing with every puff of hot air he felt.

"Listen," Cassidy said after bagging the evidence. "Why don't you two stay at my place tonight? We have two extra bedrooms. I know you can't stay here. It would be better if you were somewhere safe, at least until we have answers."

Wes glanced at Paige, who nodded.

"I'd feel better staying anywhere other than my own place," she affirmed.

"I'm going to need to fix my window before I stay here again."

"Ty is bringing some wood over," Cassidy said. "I just called him."

"Thank you."

"That's what friends are for." Cassidy glanced

back and forth between them. "You two doing okay? It's quite the day you're having. The week, for that matter."

"I, for one, am just happy to be alive," Paige said.

Cassidy nodded. "I can imagine. We've been taking Jennifer's photo around to various business owners and rental agencies to see if anyone recognizes her. So far, I haven't had any luck."

"Certainly, someone here on the island has seen her," Wes said. "She's not a ghost. She launched that boat from somewhere."

"As far as I know, the only time someone can confirm seeing her was in Lisa's that day. As soon as we're able to locate her, we'll bring her in for questioning."

"What about the boat that hit us?" Wes asked. "Any leads on that?"

"Not yet. We've been at the marina talking to people. We're hopeful that someone will come forward who saw something."

"It's like she's invisible," Wes said. "It just doesn't seem possible that she's getting away with this."

"I'm sorry." Cassidy frowned, compassion staining her eyes. "I know it has to be terribly frustrating for you."

"I just don't want to see anyone get hurt." Paige. He mostly didn't want to see Paige get hurt.

"None of us do."

Wes rubbed his jaw. He had to think of a plan to keep Paige safe.

Just as the thought entered his mind, an idea hit him and he straightened. He replayed some of the things Paige had told him today. He remembered hearing her talk, hearing her share about the things in life that were valuable to her. Things that might convince her to put her safety first.

His idea was risky. It could totally backfire.

But it was worth pursuing.

His plan could save Paige's life . . . and that was the most important thing. He only prayed that she would forgive him.

CHAPTER SEVENTEEN

PAIGE HAD SLEPT BETTER than she expected in the spare bedroom at Cassidy and Ty's place. It helped knowing that Wes, the police chief, and a former Navy SEAL were in the same house.

She'd awoken as the sunlight filtered through the blinds and into the room. On the other side of the house, she could hear murmuring and dishes clanging together. Obviously, other people were up. But she wasn't quite ready.

Instead, she drew in a deep breath. Memories of yesterday filled her mind.

Memories of the boat crash. Of almost kissing Wes. Of hearing that brick shatter the window.

Scary. Wonderful. Scary.

Her life was never simple. No, it had always been

a sandwich of good times and bad times. Her stay here in Lantern Beach was no different.

She pressed her head into the pillow. What was she going to do? Would Jennifer keep coming after her if she stayed here? How would everything end?

She had no idea. But she did know she had a job to do.

After getting dressed, she stepped into the kitchen. Everyone sat around the table, enjoying some yogurt parfaits and coffee.

Her gaze met Wes's, and she felt her cheeks heat. There was no reason for her to react this way. Yet she couldn't deny that she was drawn to the man.

"Good morning." She pushed a curl behind her ear.

"Morning," Ty said. "Help yourself. These blueberries are out of this world. Got them from Skye's produce stand."

Paige lowered herself into an empty chair, realizing that everything felt oddly normal. She desperately wanted to feel normal as well.

After taking a sip of her coffee, she asked, "Any updates?"

The three of them glanced at each other.

"We haven't located Jennifer yet," Cassidy said. "We're going to start the search again this morning. We're hoping for some answers."

"I'm hoping for answers also."

"We did get a lead on the boat," Cassidy continued. "A vacationer reported that he was about to launch from the harbor area. He forgot something in his car. When he returned, his boat was gone. He could see someone behind the wheel in the distance, but it was too far away to see any details."

"Did they find his boat?" Paige stuck her spoon into the yogurt, berry, granola mix.

"They did. It had been left at one of the private docks soundside. There was obviously some damage to it, but the house near the dock is currently empty."

She frowned. "In other words, no one saw anything?"

Cassidy nodded. "Right."

Another dead end.

"I think it would be better if you stayed here this morning," Cassidy continued, starting to collect the dishes from the table and carry them to the sink. "I'll get someone to cover for you at work."

"But—I have a job to do. I don't want to sit around all day in fear." That sounded awful.

"I know that doesn't sound fun," Cassidy said. "But your safety is my first concern."

Paige wanted to keep arguing and pushing her point. Before she could, someone knocked at the door.

She braced herself, halfway expecting another attack by Jennifer. But when she saw Wes exchange a glance with Cassidy, her instincts told her there was more to this story.

As Ty answered the door and then stepped back, Paige saw two familiar figures step inside.

She stood, the air leaving her lungs. "Mom? Dad? What are you doing here?"

————

PAIGE GLANCED at her mom and dad, unsure if she was seeing things or if they were really here.

But it was them.

Her mom with her short honey-blonde hair and premature wrinkles from her years out in the sun. Her dad with his nearly bald head and twenty extra pounds, mostly in his stomach area.

She'd never seen a more welcome sight.

"How did you know where I was?" Paige stepped toward them, still feeling uncertain about how they would react to seeing her. She didn't know whether to hug them or to run.

"Wes called us last night." Worry and concern etched into her mom's features. "He said you were in trouble and that we should come right away."

Paige looked back at Wes, her eyes flaring with

disbelief. This wasn't his business. He never should have interfered.

She plastered on a more pleasant expression as she turned back to her parents. "Is that right?"

Her dad reached for her arm, that same worry present in his expression. But it was his voice—wrought with something close to grief—that pummeled her heart.

"Are you okay, Paige?" he asked.

Her shoulders heaved as she stared at her dad. She held back a sob. Her dad . . . he was here . . . and he didn't look angry. Or like he hated her. Or . . . any of the other scenarios that had constantly run through her head.

"I'm . . . fine."

"I've missed you so much." Her dad's voice cracked, like he also had to hold back tears.

Her dad? Cry? She'd only ever seen that once—after his mother died. Seeing it broke her heart.

"I've missed you too, Dad." She could hardly understand her own words as her voice seemed to yelp with emotion.

The next instant, they embraced. She buried herself in her dad's arms, strong from his days of fishing and hauling in the big catches. He'd always been such a good dad, from the time he read her stories on his knee all the way until he danced with her at her cousin's wedding last fall.

Paige glanced back. Cassidy, Ty, and Kujo had disappeared—probably to the back of the house. But Wes still lingered, as if he wanted to explain.

Explain? There was no way he'd be able to explain this one.

"I can't believe you came." Paige shook her head, still feeling shell-shocked or like this was a dream.

"We drove all night."

Dark circles hung beneath her mom's eyes, the circles that clearly showcased her exhaustion, how much she'd aged in the short time since Paige had last seen her. The thought caused a ball of emotion to lodge in Paige's throat.

"We've been praying that we would hear from you," Mom whispered. "That you'd come back into our lives."

"I didn't think you wanted to talk to me after Owen . . ." Paige's voice broke. She didn't deserve her parents' forgiveness. She'd messed up so badly and caused them so much pain.

"I messed up, Paige," Dad said. "I spoke out of anger, out of hurt. I was desperate to get you to stay and thought the ultimatum would keep you at home. I'm so sorry."

"You didn't call . . ." If his words were true, why had they been silent?

"By the time we came to our senses, you'd changed your phone number."

Paige pressed her lips together. She'd gotten a new cellular plan when she'd gone to Wilmington—a cheaper one that fit her new budget. At that point, she'd figured the phone number change wouldn't matter, that her family was a part of her past.

"We'll always love you, Paige." Her dad pulled her into another hug. "We just want what's best for you. We could have handled the situation better."

Tears burned her eyes. Paige wanted to believe his words. She did. But there was so much more to the story. As much as she craved her parents' forgiveness . . . could she ever forgive herself?

"But your heart . . ." Paige's hand went over her mouth as her emotions overwhelmed her. "Can you even travel like this?"

"I'm doing much better."

"It's all my fault," Paige whispered. "If I hadn't gone with Owen, you would still be healthy right now. You'd have your business. I messed everything up!"

"Your father would have had his heart attack if you'd stayed or gone," her mom said. "Stop beating yourself up over it."

"No, Aunt Sue told me that the doctor said it was caused by stress. I was the one who stressed you out.

Who made your blood pressure skyrocket. It was my fault!"

"Aunt Sue? You talked to her?" her mom asked.

"I knew you didn't want to talk to me, so I called her. She told me I had no business being concerned for Dad, that this was all my fault . . ."

"Oh, Paige . . . Aunt Sue should have never said that."

"But it was true."

Mom shook her head. "Paige . . . we just want to take you home, dear."

Paige stepped back, shock washing over her. "Home? To Florida?"

"That's right," her mom said. "We want you to be safe. With us."

What exactly had Wes told them?

Paige turned toward Wes, her eyes blazing as she realized just how many lines he'd crossed. "Could I have a moment with you, Wes?"

His expression remained placid. "Of course."

He had no idea just how deep her story went. But he was about to find out.

And it wasn't going to be fun.

———

WES BRACED himself as Paige shut the door behind

her after they'd stepped into her temporary bedroom. He knew he'd taken a risk by doing this, but he'd had no other choice. He had to get Paige off of this island and away from danger.

"What gave you the right to call my parents?" Paige blurted. Fire lit her eyes as she faced him, looking like she was ready to fight to the death.

"I need to get you out of here and get you somewhere safe." His words sounded feeble, even to his own ears.

"That's for me to decide, not you." She jammed her finger into her chest and then his as if to emphasize her words.

He raised his hands. This was going to be worse than he imagined, and he wasn't sure how to explain himself. "I only want to help."

"You overstepped."

"What happened with your dad, Paige? With his heart?"

Her eyes welled with tears. "When I chose Owen instead of him . . . when I accused my father of falsely accusing Owen . . . it broke his heart. Literally."

Wes's heart pounded in his ears, each beat seeming to suspend time.

"He could have died," Paige continued. "The stress I put him under . . . it was too much for his body to handle. My aunt told me that he was in surgery for six hours, and doctors weren't sure he was going to make it."

A sob wracked her body as tears streamed down her cheeks. He saw the guilt she'd been carrying. The anger she held toward herself. The doubt she had about her decisions.

And suddenly everything made sense to Wes. No wonder she was so guarded. So cautious. So confused by the way Jennifer had tried to poison her thoughts.

Wes leaned closer, desperate to get through to her. "Paige, you know I care about you. I'm concerned for you. I can't have you stay here with a psycho on the loose."

"That's my choice. I've felt myself falling for you, Wes, and that's scared me to no end. But your problems can't dictate my future." Her voice rose with emotion with every word.

"You know I didn't mean it that way." If Paige would just slow down and take a minute to really think this through, maybe she'd understand . . .

"You shouldn't have called them." She raised her chin, not backing down.

Wes didn't know what else to say. He didn't regret his actions—not if they kept Paige alive. But he hated the agony in her gaze right now. "I can't apologize."

Paige stared at him a moment before shaking her head. "I don't even know what to say. I have to go out there and talk to my mom and dad. I can't do this right now."

"Do what?"

"You. Me. This."

She stormed out before Wes could say anything else.

Wes lowered his head as his heart twisted in agony. Why had doing the right thing felt so awful?

CHAPTER EIGHTEEN

WES COULD FEEL Cassidy and Ty's eyes on him as he stared out the window.

A few minutes ago, Paige had left with her parents. She'd given him a scowl. Hugged Cassidy and Ty. Patted Kujo on the head. Then she was gone, and an emptiness filled him.

"That was tough," Cassidy finally said. She stood in the background with her arms crossed, giving him space. She'd warned him how this might turn out. So had Ty.

"Tell me about it." He rubbed his jaw, wondering if all of this was a huge mistake.

"You sure you don't want to go after her?" Ty asked. "It's not too late."

"Do I want to?" Wes rubbed his neck. "Yes, more than anything. But I need her off this island until I know she's safe. Even if she hates me. At least, I know she's okay."

"I'd feel better if she'd let one of my officers escort her . . ." Cassidy said.

She'd offered, but Paige had refused. Said she was with her parents, leaving the island, so no one should come after her now.

He hoped she was right

After a moment of quiet, Cassidy stepped forward and quietly asked, "So you're ready to proceed?"

He stepped away from the window as the car disappeared. "As ready as I can be."

She held up a paper, still looking hesitant. "This is the message I think you should send to Jennifer. Then we're going to your house, and we'll wait for her. With an invitation like this, surely she'll show up."

Wes read the words on the paper.

BREAKING **up with you was the biggest mistake of my life. I need to see you again. Please. It's all I can think about.**

HE GLANCED AT CASSIDY, who'd been openly studying his expression.

"What do you think?" Cassidy asked.

He let out a long breath. "Well, it's not a lie. I suppose it just depends on what perspective you look at it from." Breaking up with her had been a mistake—it had caused heartache. Yet it had been necessary. And thinking about finding Jennifer again had been at the forefront of his mind for days now.

"Since we don't have her phone number, post it as a private message to her social media," Cassidy said. "She'll read it. Hopefully, she'll come looking for you. When she does, we'll arrest her, and all of this will be over with."

"It almost sounds too easy, doesn't it?" Wes sagged against the table.

"It's worth a try," Cassidy said. "If it doesn't work, we'll come up with Plan B."

Ty crossed his arms over his chest and leaned against the kitchen counter, his eyes narrow with thought. "Are there any new reports from anyone who's seen her around? As many things as she's done, I just can't believe she's been so much of a ghost."

"People saw her in Lisa's that day, of course," Cassidy said. "And then the man saw her pull away with his boat. But . . . otherwise she's done a great job staying under the radar."

"This island's not that big," Wes muttered. "Yet it seems entirely too easy for people to hide out here."

"I couldn't agree with you more." Cassidy straightened. "But we've got some work to do. I need to wait at your house with you, preferably without Jennifer knowing I'm there."

"Any ideas how we're going to do that?" Ty asked.

"I'll figure out a way," Cassidy said. "In the meantime, we don't have any time to lose. Let's get moving."

———

PAIGE WENT BACK to her RV and packed her things. As she did, her emotions clamored for attention inside her. She wasn't sure which one would win and get the forefront position in her heart and mind.

Betrayal—by Wes.

Anger—at being left out of the loop in all of this.

Relief—at seeing her parents and realizing they didn't hate her.

She paused from packing for long enough to close her eyes and hold her tears in. This wasn't the time for her to lose it. There would be plenty of opportunities for that later.

Right now, she needed to finish packing.

She'd really only brought a suitcase with her, her laptop computer, and a few personal items when she'd moved. It wouldn't take that long to gather everything.

When she got back to Florida, she would mail the rest of her rent and let the RV's owner know that she had moved out. He'd find a new tenant.

As she'd gathered her belongings, her parents looked around, sad expressions on their faces. They'd worked hard to purchase a small home on the water. Of course, they'd wanted better for their daughter than for her to live in an old camper. To them, this probably looked like Paige was at the lowest point of her life.

The truth was that, up until a few days ago, she'd felt on top of the world. Would her mom and dad ever understand that? Should she even bother to explain?

In the grand scheme of things, there were bigger issues at hand. There was her dad's heart attack. The fact that he could no longer work the job he'd loved because of it. The fact that all of it was her fault . . . all because she'd been so selfish.

Standing in the doorway, she looked back one last time at her "home." It hadn't been much, but she'd been happy here for a little while. Really happy.

She stepped outside and raised her suitcase. The

sunshine hit her face, and once again she was reminded of how much she would miss this place.

She forced a tight smile at her mom and dad as they shifted awkwardly in front of her.

"Let's go." Her stomach roiled as she said the words.

Her mom patted her hand, a frown pulling at the corners of her lips. "We've missed you so much, Paige."

Tears rimmed her eyes. She was so mad at Wes, yet . . . her parents were here. She'd been so certain they'd never want to see her again. Yet all the hate she'd expected was absent.

"I can't believe you'd welcome me at all." Her voice cracked as she said the words.

Her dad tilted his head, warmth filling his gaze. "Oh, Paige. You know nothing you could do will ever change that."

Paige fell into his arms, months of guilt clawing at her insides. She'd missed his hugs so much. But she didn't deserve his forgiveness. No, she deserved every moment of sadness she'd been through.

"But your heart attack . . ." she whispered.

"Paige, darling, that wasn't your fault." He pulled her closer.

She wiped beneath her eyes as moisture poured down, dampening her father's shirt. "Of course it was. I chose Owen over my family . . . after what he'd done. I chose to believe him. I was so stupid."

Her dad stepped back just far enough that Paige could look him in the eyes. "Owen was very charming. He pulled the wool over my own eyes for a long time. It's the only way he was able to steal that money from me."

"He told me that he didn't steal that money from you. That he was framed. He said you'd never liked him and were looking for a way to get rid of him. Who am I if I don't even stand up for my flesh and blood?" How could she have been so, so wrong?

Her mom rested her hand on Paige's back. "Don't be so hard on yourself. We all make mistakes, especially in our youth. Love can blind us to things."

Love can blind us to things . . . had she been blinded by Wes? Not that she was in love with him . . . it was too soon, right? They had been developing their friendship for the past month, though.

Still, it didn't matter how Paige had felt last week or even a few hours ago. Wes had betrayed her. How dare he call her parents? To think he knew what was best for her?

This should have been all her decision. And she wasn't sure how she'd ever forgive him for it.

CHAPTER NINETEEN

AN HOUR LATER, they were finally on the ferry. The line had been long, and they'd been at the end of it. They'd had some time to kill, so Paige, her mom, and her dad had walked to a little shop not far from the loading area and purchased sandwiches, bottled drinks, and bags of chips. They'd eaten outside, leaning on the hood of the car, and not saying much.

There was so much to say yet so little that was important.

Soon after, they'd pulled their cars onto the ferry, parked, and climbed out to enjoy the breeze coming off the water. The three of them stood by the railing now, waiting for the ferry to take off.

She thought maybe she'd feel relief. Feel closure. Feel something other than sadness.

But she didn't. No part of her wanted to be on this boat right now. Her soul felt too unsettled.

"You care about this Wes guy, don't you?" Her mom's gaze, once on the water, drifted back to Paige.

A bittersweet feeling fell over Paige at her words. "Yeah, I do. Unfortunately."

"If he cares about you, then he'll wait for you."

"Wait for me to what?" What was her mom talking about? Wait for her to return to her senses? To forgive him?

"He'll wait for you to return."

Paige did a doubletake. "You think I'm going to return here?"

A motherly look crossed her face, one that showed she knew her daughter more than Paige knew herself. "I think you love this place very much. I can see it in your eyes. You have friends. You made yourself a home. Found a job."

"But you and Dad aren't here . . ." Her family meant everything to her, which was why it hurt so much when she'd messed up. She'd basically been cut off from her family, and her aunt had made it clear she was no longer welcome . . . not after all the damage she'd done.

"Honey, a lot has happened since you left. The heart attack made us reevaluate things. We decided that it was time for us to retire. We sold the business and bought a camper. We're going to travel the country."

"What?" Paige blinked, certain she hadn't heard correctly.

"We're so excited. Your dad couldn't continue on with that kind of work schedule. He was just getting too old. It puts a lot of strain on the body. Probably that's why he had his heart attack. It was bound to happen."

"But . . ." She tried to process everything she'd just learned, to figure out how that changed her future.

"Paige, you're the one who has to wake up every morning and live with your choices," her dad said. "Not us. I want nothing more than to take you back home so I can know you're safe. So I can see you every day. But, my little girl, you're not so little anymore. You're a woman with her whole life ahead of her. You make the choices that you can live with."

Paige wiped away her tears, his words overwhelming her heart with both love and relief. She'd never imagined her conversation with her parents would go this way. "You mean that, Dad?"

"Of course I do." He gently patted her face. "I only want what's best for you. That's what love is, isn't it?"

She remembered Wes sending her away . . . and saying it was because she'd be safe.

Maybe he really did care about her. Was he sacrificing what he wanted in order to keep her safe?

A new emotion and determination rose in her. "Mom, Dad . . . you've always taught me not to run way from my problems."

"Right, dear." Her mom stared at her in curiosity. Behind her, the ferry workers pulled a gate across the back of the loading area.

"I can't leave here . . . not yet, at least. I have things that are unfinished. I think I'll always regret it."

"But . . ." Her dad looked at the docks. The workers there were just fastening the gate.

Paige reached up and kissed her mom's cheek and then her dad's. "I'm going to talk to you again soon. But I don't want to make one of the biggest mistakes of my life. I need to tie up some loose ends before I figure out my future. I love you both so much, and I'm so sorry for everything."

"We love you too, and you're forgiven," her dad said.

A sob welled in her. "Thank you."

"You better go!" her dad said.

Paige nodded and began weaving through the cars.

No way was her sedan getting off this boat. She grabbed her keys from her bag and tossed them to her dad. "Leave it on the ferry docks on the other side! I'll catch a ride to pick it up."

She darted toward the ferry workers and looked at them. "I have to get off of this ferry. Now."

"Lady, we're—"

"Please," she said. "Please. It's life or death. I work for the PD here."

She was throwing out everything she could—but her words were true. Jennifer had put them all in a deadly situation. She was a part of this police department. She wanted to be involved in the woman's capture and arrest.

The two ferry workers glanced at each other.

Paige wasn't sure if it was too late or not. But she prayed it wasn't.

———

WES LEANED BACK on the couch and glanced at his watch. It had been two hours since he'd sent that message to Jennifer. He knew that he shouldn't have such high expectations. It was just that he couldn't see himself waiting like this for hours on end. Definitely not for days. He knew Cassidy had other work to do, as well.

This was beginning to feel like a colossal waste of time. Even worse, he missed Paige.

He kept picturing her leaving. Glaring at him. He remembered hearing her parents' car pull away, Paige inside.

At moments, all of this felt like a big mistake. Wes felt like he should jump in his truck, drive to the docks, and hope he could catch Paige before she left.

But the reality of Jennifer remained.

Still, what if he never saw Paige again? The thought was almost more than he could handle.

Cassidy stepped into the room. She'd been working in the kitchen, making phone calls and looking at some paperwork she'd brought. A new light had filled her eyes. "Good news. I think we figured out where Jennifer is staying."

Wes straightened, ready to hear something positive. "Where?"

"There's an Airbnb at a house down on Sea Oats Drive. We didn't think to check there—we only checked with the realty companies and the inn. Anyway, someone who fits Jennifer's description has been staying at one of those private rentals. I'm sending Officer Bradshaw over there now."

Wes's heart pounded in his ears. He wouldn't allow himself to hope that Jennifer would actually be there. That seemed too easy. But maybe—just maybe

—they would catch a break here soon. Maybe all of this wouldn't be happening for nothing.

"So now we just wait?" he said.

"Now we wait." She nodded toward his phone. "Any responses?"

He glanced at his phone screen and shook his head. "No, nothing. What if Jennifer knows this is a trap?"

Cassidy pressed her lips together and shook her head, making it obvious she wasn't willing to believe that. "I think Jennifer's desperate to win you back. The first sign that you're interested . . . I think she's going to jump on it."

Wes hoped that was the case.

He imagined Paige again. Imagined the last time they were here at his place. When he'd almost kissed her—until that brick had been flung through the window.

He wanted nothing more than to beg her to come back here. To tell her how he really felt.

But he couldn't do that. Not until he knew she was safe.

He prayed this worked.

Just as he muttered another "amen," he saw a flash of movement down his lane.

He leaned into the window, hoping for a better glance.

But whatever he'd seen was gone. Had the person ducked into the woods surrounding the lane?

Was that person Jennifer?

They would find out soon enough.

"Cassidy," he called. "I think I saw something."

CHAPTER TWENTY

PAIGE KNEW she looked like a crazy woman, but she didn't care. She pedaled the bike harder, faster along the highway that cut down the length of the island.

She'd been able to rent a beach cruiser from someone down at the docks—after she'd given them a fifty-dollar deposit and a promise to return it.

Paige knew her actions might seem erratic to some, but she was determined to do this. To follow her gut instead of acting like a robot.

Her legs aching, she turned onto the lane leading to Wes's house. The sun burned her skin. There was no cloud cover today.

Any other time, she'd enjoy the feeling of the wind in her hair. But right now, she was on a mission. She hadn't even had time to call Wes. No, she wanted to just show up. Surprise him. Listen to him talk from the heart.

And she hoped he had a really good explanation.

Her tires bumped on the gravel road. Trees surrounded her on either side. When the foliage cleared, Wes's house would appear, along with four others. Beyond them was the sound.

She hoped he was home.

How would Wes react to seeing her? She had no idea. But she needed closure—or permission—to move forward.

But no more running away. No more unspoken conversations. Life was too short for that.

The thought of facing her problems brought a surge of freedom.

Not much longer and she'd be at Wes's place.

She turned with the lane as it bent toward the water.

As she did, something rammed into her head.

Everything went black, and Paige felt herself crashing onto the rocky road below.

What had just happened?

———

PAIGE PULLED HER EYES OPEN. How much time had passed? Where was she?

Everything blurred around her, and her head ached something fierce.

Someone moved near her.

She blinked. Help? Or was it the person who'd done this to her?

It was hard to know. Everything was blurry still.

"Stay away from him." A woman leered down at Paige as she lay on the ground. "Do you understand?"

A moan escaped from Paige.

Was that Jennifer? She was the only one who made sense. Or was Paige seeing things? Was any of this really happening?

"This is your last warning," the woman continued. "Next time I won't be as nice. He's mine."

Paige blinked, desperate for a clearer picture to come into view. But her head pounded so hard.

She reached for her temples, desperate to stop the pain.

She was still on the gravel road, she realized. The rocks beneath her dug into her skin. The sun bore down on her. The bike lay at her side.

But the woman . . . where had she gone?

She moved her head for a better look, but she couldn't see anything.

Had Jennifer left?

Paige didn't know. But she knew with absolute clarity she needed to get to safety . . . soon.

Because out here, she was a sitting duck. Defenseless. Unable to function.

She staggered to her feet. Now she needed to figure out where she was going. Instead, she collapsed again.

CHAPTER TWENTY-ONE

"SOMEONE WAS OUT THERE," Wes repeated, still staring out the window.

"Where did this person go?" Cassidy asked, her gaze fixated outside.

He reached for the doorknob, everything inside him screaming that something was wrong. "I'm going to go check."

"Do you really think that's a good idea?" Cassidy asked.

"I don't think Jennifer will hurt me," Wes said. "Especially not if she thinks I'm still in love with her."

Cassidy shifted, as if uncomfortable, but she didn't try to stop him. "If you're not back in five minutes, I'm going to come looking for you."

"I'd expect nothing less." Wes stepped outside

onto his deck and glanced around. His skin crawled at the feeling of unseen eyes on him.

Someone was out there.

Probably Jennifer. What he didn't know was what she was planning. But he wanted this over with.

He rushed down his steps and onto the grass below. As he did, he continually surveyed everything around him. He had to be careful. He'd meant it when he said he didn't think Jennifer would hurt him.

But Jennifer *had* crashed into his catamaran yesterday. Things could have turned out a lot differently. His ex was unpredictable, so Wes had to keep his eyes open and his guard up.

He turned from his drive and paused on the lane, near the woods surrounding the road.

His eyes widened. Someone lay on the ground, a bike sprawled beside her body.

Wes's heart thumped in his chest. Was that . . . Paige?

He rushed toward her, quickly noting the blood running down her forehead. Something bad had happened to her.

"Paige . . . " He grasped her shoulders, desperate to see with his own eyes that she was okay.

Her eyes looked glazed as she pushed herself up and rubbed her head. "Wes?"

He glanced around again, another surge of intuition telling him it wasn't safe out here. He needed to get Paige off this road.

"Come on, let's get you back to my place." Without asking permission, he reached down and scooped Paige up into his arms. Her head flopped against his shoulder, and she didn't argue.

That was the first sign she wasn't okay.

Moving quickly, Wes carried her back to his house.

Cassidy opened the door, her eyes widening when she spotted Paige. "What . . . ?"

He rushed past and laid Paige on the couch. "I found her like this on the lane, a bike beside her."

"You've got her for a minute?" Cassidy asked, reaching for the gun at her waist and stepping toward the door.

"Yeah, I've got Paige. You go after Jennifer."

Cassidy rushed out the door.

Neither of them thought this was an accident. No, Jennifer had been out there. She must have seen Paige coming and . . .

Anger snaked through his veins.

She was even more twisted than he thought, and she would stop at nothing . . . wouldn't she?

PAIGE BLINKED as everything came into focus around her. The familiar house with its wood paneling. That smell of cedarwood. Then . . . Wes.

She closed her eyes as her head began to pound furiously.

Everything that happened flooded into her mind. She'd been on her bike, less than a block away from Wes's when something had rammed into the side of her head.

"Paige, are you okay?" Wes squinted at her, worry capturing his features as he stared down at her.

She let out a soft moan, her head still pounding. "Yeah, I guess."

"Here, drink some water." He handed her a bottle.

Paige took a sip, wishing the cool liquid could wash away the pulsating pain she felt in her skull.

"I thought you were leaving," Wes said, his eyes still narrow with concern.

Paige shrugged, waiting for her mind to clear. "I was, but . . . I couldn't."

The door opened, and Cassidy stepped inside, a scowl on her face.

"She's gone," she announced.

Paige's stomach sank, though she wasn't really surprised.

"I found the stick she hit you with. We'll take that

in for evidence. I can also see where she was hiding out in the woods. The underbrush was trampled. But she must have had a car somewhere because she's clearly not here any longer."

"That's . . . disappointing," Wes muttered.

"Yes, it is." Cassidy let out a long breath before turning toward Paige. "You're here still. I thought you were on the ferry. Did something happen?"

"No." Paige rubbed her head. "It's just . . ."

"On second thought, I can tell you need to recover before I pepper you with questions," Cassidy said. "Do you need to go to the clinic?"

Paige raised her hands. "No, I'll be fine."

Cassidy's phone rang. She excused herself, muttered a few things into the device, and then returned with a new light in her eyes. "It definitely looks like Jennifer was staying at that Airbnb in town."

Paige perked at the news, her head suddenly not hurting as much. "Really? You found where she's staying?"

"I'm going to go there now and check it out myself," Cassidy said. "I want to see the place—her things—with my own eyes, see if I can figure out exactly what Jennifer has been up to."

Wes raised his hand, as if to answer a question that hadn't yet been asked. "We'll be fine here. We'll keep the doors locked, and I'll remain vigilant until I hear back from you."

With a hesitant nod, Cassidy stepped toward the door. "Call us if you need us, okay?"

"Will do," Wes said.

But Paige wasn't sure anyone would be able to help in this situation.

CHAPTER TWENTY-TWO

WES DIDN'T PRESS Paige for answers. He didn't disturb her as she lay back on the couch with her eyes squeezed closed and in obvious discomfort. She needed to focus on her recovery right now.

But they both knew the truth. Jennifer had done this to her.

Had Jennifer been on her way to his place when it happened? Disappointment bit hard. If that was the case, then they'd been close to ending all of this. Paige was supposed to be on that ferry headed back home.

What had changed her mind?

As she moaned again, Wes moved to sit beside her. She pulled herself up, and he slipped an arm around her back to offer support.

"Are you sure I can't take you to the clinic?" Wes desperately didn't want anything to happen to her.

She nodded, still flinching with every movement. "Yeah, I'll be fine. It's not even my head. It's my whole body from where I hit the ground."

"I'm sure that didn't feel good."

"How did she even know I was coming? It was almost like she was waiting for me."

Wes frowned. Paige hadn't been briefed on their plan.

Paige studied his face. "What?"

He shrugged, not wanting to put any additional stress on her. "Nothing."

"No, there is something. Tell me what."

"It's not important . . ."

She touched his arm. "I feel like you're trying to protect me. Just say it."

He swallowed hard, knowing Paige wouldn't give up until he told her what was on his mind. "We set up a sting, hoping to lure Jennifer out here so Cassidy could arrest her."

Paige's head dropped forward as guilt washed over her features. "But I ruined it."

Wes squeezed her arm, wanting more than anything to ease her anguished thoughts. "You didn't know."

"But I was supposed to be on that boat."

"Like I said, you didn't know."

She raised her head, but her eyes were still closed. "So, I left Florida and that resulted in my dad having a heart attack. I was determined not to make the same mistake, so I decided not to run this time. However, that also proved to be a big mistake."

"Paige . . ." Wes wanted to say the right thing, to make her feel better . . . but he wasn't sure how to do that. He left his hand on her arm, desperate to get through to her.

She stood, wobbling as she did. She grabbed the wall to steady herself and shook her head. "You know what? I need to start making some calls about tomorrow."

"What's happening tomorrow?" He had no idea where she was going with this.

"The Lantern Beach Scrub a Dub Dub. I've got to make sure everything is lined up. If you'll excuse me . . . I could just use some time to myself."

Wes frowned. He understood. He really did.

He only wished he hadn't brought all of this anguish upon her.

———

PAIGE STRAIGHTENED when she heard the door opening an hour later.

Was it Cassidy? Had she discovered something?

Paige put her pen and paper down on the kitchen table, where she'd been working in an effort to distract herself. She wanted to talk to Wes about things, but not like this. Not with her thoughts so muddled.

Not only was her head pounding from the attack, but it also pounded because she'd been staring at her notes for the past hour. She knew everything was lined up, but that didn't stop her from reviewing each detail for tomorrow's event over and over again.

It was better than facing Wes. Better than owning up to the fact that she'd ruined their plan. If she hadn't come down the road when she did . . . Jennifer might be in custody right now. How did she come to terms with that realization?

Cassidy stepped inside and remained near the door, almost like a messenger might. Paige held her breath as she waited to hear what Cassidy had discovered. She prayed it wasn't another dead end.

"Good news," Cassidy said. "Jennifer was staying at that Airbnb."

Wes stood from the couch and stepped closer to Cassidy. "Was she there?"

Cassidy frowned. "No, we weren't that lucky. The owner of the house hasn't seen her since early this morning. Said she was very quiet, minded her own business, and seemed friendly."

"Was she staying by herself?" Paige asked.

"Yes, she was. Why?"

"When Jennifer talked to me at Lisa's place, she said she was here with her husband on a vacation." She'd even had a ring. She'd been convincing.

"She probably used that as part of her story to make herself sound more believable," Cassidy said. "Nothing we've discovered has led us to believe she's married."

"Good to know," Paige muttered.

"But this is what we did find." Cassidy held her phone up.

Paige stood from the kitchen table and stepped closer for a better look. Cassidy had taken photos of the inside of the place. Pictures had been spread across one of the dressers there.

Pictures of Paige and Wes—except in each photo Paige's face had been crossed out with a fat black marker. There was a snapshot of them at the beach playing in the water. Another of them on the deck outside of Paige's RV. Another of them watching the sunset at a nearby waterside park.

She sucked in a breath as she realized just how serious this was—as if she didn't already know. But this woman was messed up. Full of lies. Desperate enough to hurt others. Unbalanced.

Wes touched her elbow, as if trying to make her feel better.

But there would be no cheering her up after seeing these. That woman had lost her mind. She must have been here at least a week, based on some of the pictures.

And Paige hadn't had a clue.

"This is disturbing." Wes's voice sounded flat, almost defeated—which was entirely unlike him.

"It is," Cassidy agreed. "But we know she's here. She can't hide but for so long. We're going to catch her."

"And in the meantime?" Paige sat back on the couch and pulled a pillow onto her lap.

Cassidy offered a sympathetic smile. "Then we wait."

CHAPTER TWENTY-THREE

WES AND PAIGE went back to Cassidy and Ty's that evening. It seemed safer than spending the night in their respective homes.

Jennifer hadn't been sighted, but Wes felt sure she was still here on Lantern Beach. Still watching. Still waiting for just the right opportunity. They'd learned through other cases that there were a lot of places to hide on this island.

He was really hoping for just a moment alone to talk to Paige. To figure out what she'd been thinking when she came back. To try to set her mind at ease.

Instead, the four of them had eaten together. Ty, who loved to cook, had fixed some chicken on the grill along with roasted potatoes and a salad. As they'd eaten dinner, things had almost felt normal—

eerily normal. They all knew things were anything *but* normal.

Clearly some tension still stretched between Wes and Paige. Would she forgive him for calling her parents?

He wasn't sure.

They finally had a moment alone after Cassidy and Ty went to bed.

Paige glanced up at him. They'd been at the table, playing cards. Now that it was just the two of them, she looked uncertain, like she should flee for bed before they got wrapped up in a conversation she didn't want to have.

He reached his hand across the table, almost as if offering an olive branch. "Paige, can we talk?"

She stared at him a moment, the cut near her temple a stark reminder of how dire this situation was. Finally, she shrugged. "I suppose."

He nodded toward the couch. Wordlessly, they both stood, walked across the room, and sat. The tension in the air was nearly physical.

He cleared his throat and tried to find the right words. "Why did you come back, Paige?"

Wes stared at her, watching her response carefully. If Jennifer hadn't knocked her off her bike, what would have happened today? Had she come back to give Wes a piece of her mind? Or to say something else?

She licked her lips. "I came back because I didn't want to run away from my problems."

"But your safety is on the line."

"You and I both know that if I left, there was a good chance I wouldn't be coming back. There was a chance that Jennifer would leave you alone. That things would feel fine. But they won't be fine unless she's locked up."

"I don't want to put you at risk."

"I don't want to be at risk either." She shivered and grabbed a blanket from the back of the couch. She pulled it over her legs and leaned back, the dim room masking some of her features. "But I'm tired of running, Wes."

Wes reached for her, desperate to comfort her, but Paige pulled away. He dropped his hand.

"Just because I came back doesn't mean I've forgiven you." Her words were quiet and her gaze nearly hollow.

"Paige, I—"

"Don't." She shook her head, her anger mellowing. "I know what you're going to say. That you were trying to look out for me. It wasn't your decision, though."

"It wasn't your choice to have a stalker after you either." How could he get through to her?

"But I'm a big girl. I can make my own choices, even if they're choices you don't like."

Wes opened his mouth and then shut it again.

"I've made mistakes in my past, Wes," she continued. "I guess we both have. But my goal isn't to look at the past and revel in my wrongdoings. I want to look forward. I want to figure out the rest of my life. Maybe not all of it. But at least the near future."

"I understand that."

She crossed her arms, needing to speak her mind. Keeping her emotions inside would do neither of them any good. "And, furthermore, you shouldn't have called my parents."

"You're right. I should have let you decide. I'm sorry, Paige." Wes thought he'd made the right choice. But listening to her now . . . he could have handled it better.

She nodded and stood. She had her apology, and now she appeared to be done. "Thank you. Now, I need to go to bed. Maybe we can talk more tomorrow, after I've had some time to let my thoughts settle."

"Of course."

Wes wondered if he'd made the biggest mistake

of his life . . . and, if he had, he had no idea if this mistake was even fixable.

PAIGE PRESSED her face into her pillow and swallowed back her tears. Why did everything have to be so complicated? How had things gone from great to so awful in just a matter of days?

She sniffled and let out a deep breath. She was going to have to deal with it. She was a grown woman, and she needed to figure out the rest of her life.

Would it be here in Lantern Beach? Should she go back to Florida?

What did she want to do with her life? There was a part of her that loved working for the Lantern Beach PD. Cassidy was a great boss. The community was a mix of peaceful and easygoing at times, and at other times crime-riddled. It made it just interesting enough to not be boring, but not so interesting that she didn't feel safe.

She blew out another breath. She should know better than to try to map out her future. It never worked that way.

We can make our plans, but the Lord determines our steps. ~Proverbs 16:9

That verse had been on a painting hanging on the wall in her parents' house.

It was true. She could make all the plans she wanted, but that didn't mean things would happen the way she desired. Part of life and being an adult was learning to roll with the punches.

Which brought her back to Wes.

His image flashed in her mind. His glimmering eyes, rakish grin, sturdy build.

How had he gained a place so quickly in her heart? And what about the overbearing decision he'd made for her, calling her parents and ultimately trying to get her off the island?

Still, she'd seen honest concern in his eyes. He said he did it because he cared about her.

But it had been intrusive. It had crossed a line.

Paige squeezed her eyes shut.

She would get some sleep. She would oversee the Lantern Beach Scrub a Dub Dub tomorrow. Then she'd figure out the rest of her life.

CHAPTER TWENTY-FOUR

WES SOMEHOW NEEDED to convince Paige to stay out of the line of fire today. However, last time he'd tried to convince her to do something, it hadn't gone over well.

He knew he couldn't tell Paige what to do. He'd learned from his past mistakes. But he prayed she had enough sense not to try to go out there today at the cleanup event and make herself an easy target. Couldn't she still be in charge from the safety of Cassidy and Ty's home?

A bad feeling churned in his gut.

He swallowed another sip of coffee, but the liquid tasted like acid in his stomach. Cassidy had already left. She had to go into the office this morning before the cleanup began. Ty was checking on his cabanas outside in preparation for another retreat. And Paige hadn't stirred yet.

At that thought, a footstep sounded behind him. He turned.

Paige stepped from the hallway. His heart skipped a beat when he saw her.

She'd showered and changed already into some black shorts and a tank top. Her face looked fresh, her curls springy, and her eyes brighter.

When he saw her flip-flops on, he knew without a doubt she was going to try to go out today.

He resisted a sigh and reminded himself that he could trust her. That he couldn't make her decisions for her. That she was a fully capable woman.

"Good morning." His throat felt tight as he said the words.

"Good morning." She grabbed a coffee mug and poured herself some coffee, still looking a little stiff. "You need more?"

He looked at his half-full cup and shook his head. The liquid already wasn't settling well in his stomach. "No, I'm okay. How are you feeling? Is your head still sore?"

"No, it's not. I think a good night's rest was the perfect medicine."

"Good. I'm glad you're doing better."

She sat down beside him and stared at him over the rim of her coffee cup. "Anything new this morning?"

He shrugged, wishing he had something to tell her. "Not that I've heard."

Her shoulders seemed to deflate. "That's too bad."

"Yes, it is. I was hoping that Jennifer would have been located by now." He wanted to ask Paige about her plans for today. But he swallowed the words. He'd wait until she brought it up, not wanting to seem pushy.

Behind them, the door opened. Cassidy stepped inside, a grin stretched across her face. "Guess what I just found out? Jennifer's car was spotted on the ferry first thing this morning. I wish the crews had realized it sooner, but there was a changeover in staffing and the new guys hadn't been briefed about Jennifer yet. Anyway, the supervisor checked the surveillance photos and spotted her car. It looks like she left the island."

Wes felt himself rising up from his seat. "Are you sure?"

"We're fairly certain," Cassidy said. "Of course, we'll double-check everything. But maybe she finally realized that she wouldn't get away with this, and she left. We'll have police tracking her in other parts of the state, but it could mean good news for you, Paige. You too, Wes. Maybe you can finally sleep at night and get on with your lives."

Wes and Paige exchanged a look full of hope . . . and some doubt.

Could Jennifer have really gotten the hint and left?

Part of him didn't want to believe it.

But that would be great news if it was true. He just needed a little more confirmation first.

———

PAIGE FELT excitement welling up in her. She wouldn't have to sit in hiding all day. Jennifer was gone—most likely.

"I can go and supervise the cleanup day," she announced, rising to her feet. "Which is great because if I have to stay inside anymore, I'm going to lose my mind."

Wes and Cassidy exchanged a glance.

"What?" she asked, confused by their hesitation. "If Jennifer's gone, there's no reason for me to stay out of sight until it's all over . . . right?"

"In theory, yes." Cassidy's smile dimmed. "We are still confirming things, of course."

Paige wasn't ready to back down. "How about this? I'll stick with Wes today. That way, both of us will have our eyes open. I'll be in public, directing people, for the most part. I should be okay, as long as I don't go anywhere alone."

"It's your call, Paige. You can do whatever you feel safest doing." Cassidy's voice still held an edge of concern.

Paige nodded, her mind made up. "I'm going then. This is my event. I want to be there to oversee it. I don't want this woman to dictate my life."

Wes stood. "I'll take you up on your offer. I'll stick with you today, just to be on the safe side."

"Absolutely." Paige glanced at her watch, feeling more excited than she had in days. "I've got to get moving. Wes, how much time do you need before you're ready?"

"Just a few minutes."

Her mind raced through everything she needed to do for today's event—in person now and not over the phone. "Great. I'll meet you back here again in five. I've got to go grab a few things myself. This is going to be the best beach cleanup event ever."

She glanced at Wes and Cassidy again. Neither of them seemed to share her excitement. But that was okay. Because she was going to make the most out of this situation.

Jennifer had left. That was great news.

But, if they were wrong . . . well, Paige didn't want to think about it.

CHAPTER TWENTY-FIVE

SOMEONE LET Paige use their golf cart. She, with Wes by her side, drove all throughout the island, monitoring the cleanup activities.

Forty bags of trash had already been collected. Mostly, it was bottles and food wrappers and illegal fireworks. There were also several cinder blocks, old tires, and some beach equipment that had blown out to sea before getting washed to shore. Huge trucks had been brought in to haul it all away

This was not only going to help the beach look more beautiful, but these efforts would also help the wildlife in the area. So much of this litter could harm or even kill them.

It felt good to be doing her part.

Paige glanced over at Wes. He scanned everything around them still, just as he'd been doing all day.

They'd seen no signs of trouble. No signs of Jennifer.

Good.

Because every time Paige thought about the woman, her head began to throb uncontrollably.

Jennifer was crazy. Certifiably. Why else would she have swung that stick out and hit Paige in the head? And what about the photos Cassidy had found in the room where she'd been staying? That woman had been watching her and Wes for several days.

Paige shivered at the thought.

"You still doing all right?" Wes asked, his gaze scanning the crowds on the boardwalk.

He'd been watching Paige also. No doubt he'd seen her shiver just now. Part of her resented it, and the other part of her delighted in his concern. It was nice to know someone was watching out for her.

"I'm great." Paige used her strongest voice. At the first sign she wasn't doing okay, Wes would probably try to find an excuse to get her back to Cassidy's place and under lock and key.

That was the last thing she wanted.

"I'd say today has been successful," he said.

Paige smiled. "Me too. I think this would be nice as an annual event."

"Only if you're here to head it up."

Paige's cheeks flushed at his words. So he wanted her to stick around? Yet he'd tried to get rid of her also. He was so confusing . . . and, at times, infuriating.

Part of Paige wanted to share all her feelings with the man and never leave his side. The other part held back, desperate to see more flaws. To realize early on why they shouldn't be together.

Her walkie talkie buzzed, and she answered. It was her crew working in the Pamlico Sound. They'd found some old motors, anchors, and other hazardous items that could seriously hurt people if they stepped on them or fell onto them while tubing or waterskiing.

They needed more manpower, people who were comfortable snorkeling or scuba diving. People who had the strength to pull some of these heavy objects out. Just as she was about to tell the water supervisor that she didn't have anyone else who could help, Wes spoke up.

"I can help."

"Really?" Paige expected Wes to want to stay out in public for only as long as necessary.

He shrugged, looking laid-back—though she knew he was anything but. "Yeah, I mean, they need help. I'm qualified. As long as we're not out there alone . . . our chances are probably better on the water anyway. At least you can see people coming."

"We should be safe . . . especially if Jennifer really did leave the island." Why did Paige sound so uncertain as she said the words?

But the fact was, if Paige was out in the water, she should be okay. Most of the areas where they were working were shallow. Jennifer wouldn't manage to get a speed boat in water at that depth. Any other boat, they would see coming.

"Okay then," she finally said. "If you don't mind helping, let's head out there. I'd love to get some pictures anyway of that part of the cleanup so we can post them to social media."

"Let's go then."

———

WES DIDN'T NEED to gear up for the area where he'd be working. The water was only about three and a half feet deep. The location could be managed by walking out, but gear was needed to see what was beneath the water in order to remove any objects they found. He was amazed by the trash he'd discovered in the sound before this. People thought they could dump things beneath the water and get away with it. Unfortunately, it was a huge safety risk.

As someone who worked out on these waters, he tried to do periodic checks in the areas he frequented. But it was a big undertaking—more than one person could handle. The Pamlico Sound was the second largest estuary on the East Coast, right behind Chesapeake Bay. In other words, it was massive.

Thankfully, the water was shallow for nearly a mile out, which made it easier to navigate.

One of the volunteers let Paige use his motorboat. Sections of the water had been blocked out on a map so volunteers would know where to work.

"You sure you're good with this?" Paige asked as they idled to a stop.

He adjusted the mask on his face. "I'm sure."

"Okay. Be careful." Her face looked pensive, like she was having second thoughts.

"I don't have to do this . . ." If Paige was uncomfortable, Wes would stay right beside her. Go back to the golf cart. Whatever made her feel safe.

"Tommy and Jake are in a boat not far from here. I can call them for help if I need to. Besides, you'll be coming up for air enough that I'll be able to communicate with you."

He nodded. She was right. There wasn't much risk being out here. And he truly hoped that Jennifer had finally gotten frightened and left the island. Any sane person would.

The problem was she wasn't exactly sane.

Wes jumped into the water, ready to use his snorkel to find the areas that needed to be cleaned up. Once he found problem areas, he could adjust his location, take off his snorkel, and dive deeper to retrieve anything he needed.

With one last wave at Paige, he put his snorkel in his mouth and disappeared into the water.

Beneath the surface, eel grass waved with the current. A stingray swam by not too far away. Tiny schools of minnows darted past.

It was like an entirely different world under here. It was beautiful and peaceful and a true sanctuary.

Wes swam around near the boat, determined to stay close.

He grabbed a broken bottle, some broken crab pods, and a few other miscellaneous things and stuck them in a mesh bag he'd brought down with him.

As he swam around another patch of grass, an old anchor came into view. He studied it a moment. This was definitely a hazard. The ends were sharp and rusted. If someone fell into the water and landed on this . . . it wouldn't be pretty.

He came to the surface a moment and handed his bag to Paige.

"How's it going?" She peered down at him from above.

"Good, but I need to pull an old anchor up. Can you move the boat about twenty feet to the west?"

"Will do." She cranked the engine and puttered the boat in the direction he'd indicated. He held onto the side and glided through the water.

"Any signs of trouble?" He glanced around the open expanse of water around them.

Paige shook her head, looking calm and collected. "No, it's been quiet out here."

Good. Maybe Jennifer was no longer a threat. Could they really be that lucky?

He didn't know. But he sure hoped so.

CHAPTER TWENTY-SIX

PAIGE COULDN'T STOP GLANCING around the beautiful, serene area surrounding her. She searched for any signs of trouble, but she didn't see anything but birds, gentle waves, and a few passing cotton-puff clouds.

In between remaining vigilant, she answered calls and followed up with other beach cleanup crews to check on their progress.

It was just after noon, so most of the teams were wrapping up. She'd planned a cookout on the beach for the volunteers. Lisa had offered to oversee that, so Paige knew she didn't have to worry about those details. Soon they would all be feasting.

Cassidy had checked in several times as well. Everything appeared to be going well on other parts of the island. There hadn't been any problems today —thank goodness.

Paige should feel on top of the world. So why did she still feel nervous?

Maybe because everything felt easy. Too easy.

She shoved her doubts down and readjusted her sunglasses against the glare of the water.

She watched as Wes went underwater. He worked to set up lines that would pull the old anchor to the surface. He said it wasn't especially heavy, but incredibly awkward. He disappeared beneath the surface again and again as he set things up.

Her phone rang, and Paige saw it was Cassidy. She took a sip of water before answering.

Her boss had been using the walkie talkies for most of the day. Why was she calling now?

"Hi, Chief. What's up?" Paige answered, her gaze scanning the horizon in anticipation of trouble.

"Paige . . . I just got an update from a state trooper. They've been trying to track down Jennifer's car all day, since she got off the ferry."

"Okay. . ."

"And it looks like Jennifer paid a tourist here on the island to impersonate her. This woman drove Jennifer's car on the ferry, just to throw us off it appears. But the woman wasn't Jennifer. She doesn't know where Jennifer is, for that matter."

Paige's heartrate accelerated.

Of course. She was correct when she'd thought things had been too easy. Now she and Wes might still be in danger.

"Where are you, Paige?" Cassidy asked.

She glanced back at land, which was a good half mile away. "We're on the water around Milepost 17, near the lighthouse. Wes's usual launching spot."

"Come back to shore ASAP. I'm going to go out there and meet you myself. I need to know the two of you are safe."

"As soon as Wes comes up to the surface again, I'll tell him. We'll take the boat back to shore and wait for you."

"Okay, I'll see you soon."

Paige glanced down at the water where Wes worked. She needed to get his attention.

Now.

———

WES TIGHTENED another rope around the anchor and backed away. Everything looked good to go, but he still needed to wrap the rope around one more side of the rusty metal first. Then they'd pull the anchor from the water instead of trying to lift it himself and risk getting cut.

His foot hit something, and he glanced down and saw a metal rod there. It almost looked like an old crowbar that had been left and buried. He added that to his list of things to take to the surface. But first, he needed to finish working on this anchor.

He'd been holding his breath underwater in an effort to get this done efficiently. There was no air tank required. But he needed to go to the surface soon and fill his lungs before he could finish securing the anchor.

Maybe when this was over, he would admit everything to Paige. He would tell her how he felt. Stop holding back.

He would be a fool to let someone like Paige walk away. Now that he'd fallen for her, there was no turning back. He'd wasted a lot of time already, and he regretted that. He needed to tell her how much he cared.

And he would.

Tonight after this was done, he decided. After the cleanup efforts were complete. When Paige would be more relaxed.

The truth was, Wes could see the two of them building a nice life together here on Lantern Beach. She shared his values. She didn't care about money or material possessions. Living a full life was entirely more important than accumulating stuff.

He wrapped the rope around the anchor in one more place and tied a knot there. As he did, his lungs tightened again, reminding him he needed air.

He had to get to the surface. He couldn't work underwater any longer without getting a breath.

As he started up, something pricked his arm. He flinched.

Blood seeped from a cut on his bicep.

Blood?

Had Wes accidentally scraped himself on the anchor?

No, he wasn't close enough to injure himself. He'd been careful.

So what had happened?

As he watched the red streaks of blood mix with the water, he felt another pierce on his other arm.

He glanced behind him and saw something shoot past. Was that . . . a spear that plunged into the sandy bottom of the sound?

A spear?

It was one that was used for spear fishing, he realized. Someone had shot that from a gun.

But . . . who?

He jerked his head back around just in time to see someone dart behind a large bed of seaweed.

He didn't have to see her face to know the truth.

It was Jennifer.

Jennifer had found him.

She was in the water.

And she was done playing games. This time, she wanted to end this . . . even if it meant hurting Wes.

Or maybe *especially* if it meant hurting Wes.

CHAPTER TWENTY-SEVEN

PAIGE SAW the commotion beneath the water. The turbulence. A disturbance in the rhythm of the current.

What was going on? Even more—how could she help without getting herself hurt?

Her first impulse was to jump in. But she couldn't see beneath the surface. Who knew what she'd be facing? Sharks sometimes wandered into these waters. Or what if Wes had gotten caught underwater somehow while trying to string up the anchor? What if he needed help?

Or what if . . . Jennifer had found them?

Paige wasn't sure how Jennifer would have done that. But she wouldn't put it past the woman.

Making a split-second choice, Paige grabbed a paddle and pushed the boat closer to the commotion.

Just as she did, a head emerged from the surface.

Wes.

He gasped in a deep breath of air and threw his goggles off.

Something was wrong. Really wrong.

Before Paige could ask him what had happened, another face emerged only a couple feet away.

Jennifer. Only her dark hair was gone. Blonde hair —just like in the pictures Wes had shown her— dripped around her face.

The woman tore off her snorkel gear and held up a gun.

A gun?

A spear gun, Paige realized. Her dad had used them on occasion, so she recognized it.

Wes's hand went to one of his arms. Blood dripped from a cut. More blood seeped from a matching wound on his other arm.

He'd been injured. Cut with one of the sharp ends of the spear?

Panic raced through her.

"You thought you were going to get away with all of this, didn't you?" Jennifer said.

Her face had taken on a new look. Gone was the scorned woman who wanted to protect other poten- tial "victims" of Wes's violent ways. This woman's nostrils flared, her eyes were wide and showed strong emotions—misplaced passion. Her teeth were clenched.

"Jennifer, you don't have to do this." Wes bounced his hands in the air as if to say, calm down.

"Yes, I do. I gave you the chance to come back to me. But that was never real, was it? You never wanted me back." Jennifer's nostrils flared.

"Jennifer, why don't you put the spear gun down and we can talk?" Wes said, his voice still placating.

"I'm beyond talking," she growled, her hand gripping the gun. "I gave you the one chance. And now it has to end."

"Jennifer . . ."

"Stop Jennifering me! I don't want to hear it. You and I were supposed to be together."

Paige watched, holding her breath. Where was everyone? The other volunteers had just been in another boat within eyesight. And Cassidy? How much longer until she arrived?

They needed help and they needed it now. But all Paige saw was an open expanse of water.

"We didn't work out," Wes said. "That happens with relationships sometimes. We only dated a month."

Paige looked around, trying to find something to help them. She had a first aid kit in the boat. An oar. A walkie talkie.

Cassidy was on her way. But would she get here in time? Besides, Cassidy would need to get out to them on the water. Jennifer would see her coming.

Despair clamped down hard inside her.

Paige needed to think of something. But she wasn't sure if inserting herself into the conversation would help or hinder the situation. Seeing Paige might only fuel Jennifer's anger.

"Let Paige go," Wes said, blood still running down his arms. "She never did anything to you."

"She was supposed to leave. Yet here she is, still hanging around." Jennifer glanced at Paige, her wide eyes showing instability. "I'm sorry, Paige. You seem nice. But you can't take a hint."

"She didn't do anything," Wes repeated. "I'm the one you have the problem with."

"I need you to stop talking!"

Paige froze. Just what was this woman's plan? To kill them both and then escape before she got caught?

A shiver went up her spine. It was the only thing that made sense. The whole "If I can't have you no one can" type of mentality.

Paige had to think of something.

Now.

Before this water became their graves.

WES FELT his panic rising as he realized the difficulty of the situation.

Jennifer had murder in her eyes. And there was nowhere to run for shelter out here. Only the water—which her spear gun could slice right through.

How had she even gotten back to the island? How had she found them? How had she gotten over here without anyone noticing?

He didn't know.

"All I wanted was you, Wes," Jennifer said, her voice trembling with emotion. "Was that too much?"

"Jennifer, you need to put the gun down." That was his first priority. He had to get that weapon away from her.

"I don't want to put the gun down!" Her voice rose. "I want to finish this."

"How are you going to finish this?" He almost didn't want to ask the question. But he had to know. He had to figure out her plan.

"You've got to die." Jennifer stared at him still, not a hint of humor on her face. She meant the words. She'd come here dead set on killing him.

In fact, if she'd been a better shot under water, he might be dead right now. Instead, those spears had just brushed his arms.

"There are better ways," Wes said, careful to keep

his voice even. "You don't have to end this with death."

"You don't understand." Her voice climbed. "I've tried to forget about you. To pretend we didn't happen. To move on. I can't. This is the only thing that makes sense. It's the only way I'll have closure."

"Jennifer, you and I both know that's not true." Wes stepped closer, playing with the idea of grabbing her gun. But that could backfire. He had to be careful. "There are other ways. You can get help."

"I don't need help! I just needed you! But everyone leaves me. My dad. My mom. Then you. I needed forever with you! And don't tell me we can make it work. You never looked at me the way you looked at her." Jennifer glared at Paige.

Wes glanced back at Paige but only for a second. Her skin had gone pale. Her eyes were wide. Her gaze was fastened on the scene in front of her.

She could try to get away. Turn the motor on. Speed away.

But it wouldn't work. He knew that just as well as Jennifer did.

Wes had to figure out some way to get out of this situation and to keep Paige alive.

"You beat yourself up, didn't you?" Paige asked, her eyes on the spear gun. "In those photos. You wanted me to believe that Wes had done it. But he would never do that to a woman."

She shrugged, unfazed. "Desperate times call for desperate measures. What can I say?"

"Jennifer—" Wes started.

"Enough talking!" She raised her gun, the end pointed at his heart. "I'm sorry, Wes. This isn't the way I wanted this to end."

"Jennifer—"

She adjusted the gun, her finger on the trigger.

Wes braced himself for the impact.

CHAPTER TWENTY-EIGHT

PAIGE KNEW she had to act and quickly. She could only think of one thing to do. She raised her oar and swung it like a bat, hitting Jennifer on the head.

The woman dropped her spear gun, thrown off guard.

The next instant, Wes dove under water—looking for the speargun, no doubt.

Jennifer opened her eyes, and anger shot from her gaze. Anger at Paige.

Oh, no.

Paige glanced down, looking for something else to defend herself with. The oar had fallen into the water behind her.

Before she could grab anything, Jennifer reached the boat. Pushed on the side until it began tipping over.

Paige tried to balance herself. But it was too late. She fell into the water.

Jennifer tackled her. Pressed on her shoulders. Plunged her underwater. Held her there.

A surge of panic raced through Paige as she lost control. She couldn't panic. She had to think clearly.

That's what her dad had always taught her to do in emergencies—and while on the water.

She had to stay focused.

Jennifer continued to press down on her shoulders, determined to hold her under until water filled her lungs.

Paige opened her eyes and glanced around beneath the murky surface.

Wes swam in the distance. He grabbed the spear gun and looked back.

His eyes went to her, widening.

He torpedoed himself through the water toward them, and his arms went around Jennifer. He pulled her off, allowing Paige to shoot back to the surface. She sucked in a quick breath of air, her body weak with fear.

She didn't have long. This situation was far from over.

Water splashed beside her.

Jennifer was fighting Wes, Paige realized.

They surfaced long enough for Wes to moan.

Then they both fell back into the water, still struggling.

Where was the spear gun? Paige needed to find it. That gun . . . it would be deadly. Whoever had it would have control.

Paige took a deep breath and went back underwater.

Wes and Jennifer wrestled only a couple feet away.

Her gaze searched the bottom of the water. The spear gun was nowhere in sight.

But a piece of metal near her feet caught her gaze. Was that a . . . crowbar?

It was small enough to lift. But heavy enough to use.

Paige grabbed it and turned back toward the scene just as Jennifer raised the speargun again.

She raised it. Toward Wes. Her finger remained poised on the trigger.

Without wasting any more time, Paige swung the crowbar, giving it every ounce of strength she had left inside her.

It hit Jennifer on the back of the head, and she went limp.

The speargun fell from her hands, dropping to the wet sand below.

Wes's gaze met hers, and he nodded his appreciation.

He wrapped his arms around Jennifer and brought her limp body to the surface. As he did, Paige grabbed the speargun.

She broke through the water and sucked in another breath.

Cassidy and Officer Bradshaw pulled up in a police boat beside them.

Help was here.

Maybe this finally was over.

For real this time.

At least, Paige prayed that was the case.

————

THE NEXT SEVERAL hours were a blur.

Wes had gone to the clinic and gotten ten stitches —six in one arm and four in the other.

Jennifer had been arrested. She'd all but admitted to doing everything, without apology. Wes wasn't sure if she'd go to jail or if she'd get help. Part of him hoped she'd do both.

The woman had tried to kill him and Paige. She was a danger to society right now. Maybe that would change one day. But she had a long way to go.

Thankfully, Cassidy had sensed something was

wrong and had come out in a boat to help. Between that and Paige's quick thinking, the situation had turned out okay.

But it could have turned out so much differently. Wes was grateful for the happy ending.

And he was anxious to see Paige again.

She'd been giving her statement to Cassidy last he heard.

He wanted to see with his own eyes that she was okay. To tell her how sorry he was again. To hopefully make things right.

It had been close out there. Really close. *Too* close.

Doc Clemson stepped into the room. "It looks like you're good to go. Just watch those cuts for any sign of infection."

"Will do."

He cast a concerned expression toward Wes. "You do realize that if that spear had gone four inches to the left or right that you wouldn't be here right now, right?"

Wes nodded. The cold reality of the situation hadn't left him. It wouldn't for a long time. "I do realize that. I'm thankful that Jennifer was such a bad shot."

"I'm glad you're okay. There's someone in the hallway who's waiting to see you."

His heart skipped a beat.

Paige. He wanted more than anything for it to be Paige waiting for him there.

"Thanks again, Doc." Wes hopped down from the examination table.

Now he was going to do what he should have done right from the start.

He was going to tell Paige how he felt, and he prayed she felt the same way.

CHAPTER TWENTY-NINE

PAIGE STOOD when the door opened. She nodded to Doc Clemson as he scurried past, trying not to show her disappointment. She'd been hoping for Wes. She'd been anxious to see him since everything that had transpired.

Just as she sank back down into the stiff seat outside the room, someone else stepped out. Paige sucked in a breath.

Wes.

She felt her eyes light up upon seeing him. Seeing him alive. A glow had returned to his skin and a sparkle to his gaze.

She'd been so worried while they were out on the water. She'd been certain something was going to happen to him. That there would be no happy ending.

"Paige." Wes stepped toward her, a new look in his eyes. "You're here."

She stood again, feeling a momentary rush of nerves. "Of course I'm here. How are you?"

He shrugged, his gaze never leaving hers. "Sore, but I'll be okay."

She smiled. "I'm glad."

"You want to take a walk to the beach?"

She supposed the beach seemed like a better place to talk than in the hallway at the clinic. "Sure, that would be great."

"Maybe we could get that ice cream we talked about getting a few days ago before all the craziness began."

"I'd like that."

Without saying anything else, Wes took her hand into his, and they left the clinic. She'd already talked to Cassidy, so they'd been cleared. Cassidy would be in touch if needed, but with Jennifer's confession, that might not be necessary.

Instead of walking to the beach, Wes paused outside the clinic and turned toward her. The sun was beginning to set, casting hues of pink and pale blue around them.

Paige's heart skipped a beat when she saw the look in Wes's eyes.

"I know this is going to sound crazy, Paige, but I love you."

Her eyes widened, uncertain if she'd heard correctly. "What—"

"No, don't say anything else. I know I've been stupid. I know I shouldn't have let my fears hold me back. And I definitely realize that I shouldn't have tried to send you away with your parents. I know it might be too little too late. But I only did those things because I cared about you. I could have shown that so much better, though."

"Wes—"

"Wait. Just a little more. Please."

She clamped her mouth shut when she saw his earnest expression, and instead she waited.

"I can't imagine my future without you, Paige Henderson. You're everything I've ever looked for in a best friend and in a soulmate. I desperately want you to stay here with me on Lantern Beach. I want to see where you and I go together. As a couple."

A smile stretched across her face as he finally paused, but she said nothing for a minute. She needed to be certain she'd been cleared to speak. She cocked an eyebrow up before asking, "Can I talk now?"

He swallowed hard, as if he understood the

tension she felt, both inside her and between them. "I would love it if you talked now."

Her grin grew, and Cassidy's words flooded in her mind.

Sometimes, the most rewarding thing we can do is to go against the current. It's challenging. It's hard. But you can make your own way . . . and sometimes that's exactly what we need to do.

Suddenly, Paige knew exactly what she wanted for her future. It wasn't based on a whim. On other people's expectations for her. Life was short . . . and she wanted to choose which direction her future would head.

Paige cleared her throat and began, a tremble of emotion in her voice. "As you know, I've made some bad decisions in my life. But when I thought you were going to die back there, my future was the only thing I could think about. My future with you. I knew that I couldn't see my tomorrows without you by my side. I didn't mean for it to happen, but I've fallen in love with you too, Wes O'Neill."

A smile spread across his face, and he stepped closer, seemingly oblivious to anyone around them. His hands went to her waist, and he pulled her toward him. "That makes me very happy to hear."

"I'm glad." She raised her gaze to meet his.

Without any more words, he leaned toward her.

Their lips met, slowly and tentatively at first before exploding with a sweet passion that Paige didn't even realize she had inside her.

She wanted to do this forever. With Wes.

Finally, Wes stepped back, the affection in his gaze taking her breath away. He cared about her. He really did. And she cared about him also.

"Now, how about that ice cream?" He took her hand.

She laced her fingers with his. "Let's go."

Maybe second chances were possible. Maybe mistakes weren't permanent. And maybe her plans to stay here on Lantern Beach with the man of her dreams wasn't crazy after all.

And, for that, Paige was forever grateful.

ALSO BY CHRISTY BARRITT:

wrong move could lead to both her discovery and her demise. Can she bring justice to the island . . . or will the hidden currents surrounding her pull her under for good?

Flood Watch

The tide is high, and so is the danger on Lantern Beach. Still in hiding after infiltrating a dangerous gang, Cassidy Livingston just has to make it a few more months before she can testify at trial and resume her old life. But trouble keeps finding her, and Cassidy is pulled into a local investigation after a man mysteriously disappears from the island she now calls home. A recurring nightmare from her time undercover only muddies things, as does a visit from the parents of her handsome ex-Navy SEAL neighbor. When a friend's life is threatened, Cassidy must make choices that put her on the verge of blowing her cover. With a flood watch on her emotions and her life in a tangle, will Cassidy find the truth? Or will her past finally drown her?

Storm Surge

A storm is brewing hundreds of miles away, but its effects are devastating even from afar. Laid-back, loose, and light: that's Cassidy Livingston's new motto. But when a makeshift boat with a bloody cloth inside washes ashore near her oceanfront home, her detective instincts shift into gear . . . again. Seeking clues isn't the only thing on her mind—romance is heating up with next-door neighbor and former Navy SEAL Ty Chambers as well. Her heart wants the love and stability she's longed for her entire life. But her hidden identity only leads to a tidal wave of turbulence. As more answers emerge about the boat, the danger around her rises, creating a treacherous swell that threatens to reveal her past. Can Cassidy mind her own business, or will the storm surge of violence and corruption that has washed ashore on Lantern Beach leave her life in wreckage?

Dangerous Waters

Danger lurks on the horizon, leaving only two choices: find shelter or flee. Cassidy Livingston's new identity has begun to feel as comfortable as her favorite sweater. She's been tucked away on Lantern Beach for weeks, waiting to testify against a deadly gang, and is settling in to a new life she wants to last forever. When she thinks she spots someone malevolent from her past, panic swells inside her. If an enemy has found her, Cassidy won't be the only one who's a target. Everyone she's come to love will also be at risk. Dangerous waters threaten to pull her into an overpowering chasm she may never escape. Can

Cassidy survive what lies ahead? Or has the tide fatally turned against her?

Perilous Riptide

Just when the current seems safer, an unseen danger emerges and threatens to destroy everything. When Cassidy Livingston finds a journal hidden deep in the recesses of her ice cream truck, her curiosity kicks into high gear. Islanders suspect that Elsa, the journal's owner, didn't die accidentally. Her final entry indicates their suspicions might be correct and that what Elsa observed on her final night may have led to her demise. Against the advice of Ty Chambers, her former Navy SEAL boyfriend, Cassidy taps into her detective skills and hunts for answers. But her search only leads to a skeletal body and trouble for both of them. As helplessness threatens to drown her, Cassidy is desperate to turn back time. Can Cassidy find what she needs to navigate the perilous situation? Or will the riptide surrounding her threaten everyone and everything Cassidy loves?

Deadly Undertow

The current's fatal pull is powerful, but so is one detective's will to live. When someone from Cassidy Livingston's past shows up on Lantern Beach and warns her of impending peril, opposing currents collide, threatening to drag her under. Running would be easy. But leaving would break her heart. Cassidy must decipher between the truth and lies, between reality and deception. Even more importantly, she must decide whom to trust and whom to fear. Her life depends on it. As danger rises and answers surface, everything Cassidy thought she knew is tested. In order to survive, Cassidy must take drastic measures and end the battle against the ruthless gang DH-7 once and for all. But if her final mission fails, the consequences will be as deadly as the raging undertow.

LANTERN BEACH ROMANTIC SUSPENSE

Tides of Deception

Change has come to Lantern Beach: a new police chief, a new season, and . . . a new romance? Austin Brooks has loved Skye Lavinia from the moment they met, but the walls she keeps around her seem impenetrable. Skye knows Austin is the best thing to ever happen to her. Yet she also knows that if he learns the truth about her past, he'd be a fool not to run. A chance encounter brings secrets bubbling to the surface, and danger soon follows. Are the life-threatening events plaguing them really accidents . . . or is someone trying to send a deadly message? With the tides on Lantern Beach come deception and lies. One question remains—who will be swept away as the water shifts? And will it bring the end for Austin and Skye, or merely the beginning?

Shadow of Intrigue

For her entire life, Lisa Garth has felt like a supporting character in the drama of life. The designation never bothered her—until now. Lantern Beach, where she's settled and runs a popular restaurant, has boarded up for the season. The slower pace leaves her with too much time alone. Braden Dillinger came to Lantern Beach to try to heal. The former Special Forces officer returned from battle with invisible scars and diminished hope. But his recovery is hampered by the fact that an unknown enemy is trying to kill him. From the moment Lisa and Braden meet, danger ignites around them, and both are drawn into a web of intrigue that turns their lives upside down. As shadows creep in, will Lisa and Braden be able to shine a light on the peril around them? Or will the encroaching darkness turn their worst nightmares into reality?

Storm of Doubt

A pastor who's lost faith in God. A romance

writer who's lost faith in love. A faceless man with a deadly obsession. Nothing has felt right in Pastor Jack Wilson's world since his wife died two years ago. He hoped coming to Lantern Beach might help soothe the ragged edges of his soul. Instead, he feels more alone than ever. Novelist Juliette Grace came to the island to hide away. Though her professional life has never been better, her personal life has imploded. Her husband left her and a stalker's threats have grown more and more dangerous. When Jack saves Juliette from an attack, he sees the terror in her gaze and knows he must protect her. But when danger strikes again, will Jack be able to keep her safe? Or will the approaching storm prove too strong to withstand?

LANTERN BEACH PD

On the Lookout

When Cassidy Chambers accepted the job as police chief on Lantern Beach, she knew the island had its secrets. But a suspicious death with potentially far-reaching implications will test all her skills —and threaten to reveal her true identity. Cassidy enlists the help of her husband, former Navy SEAL Ty Chambers. As they dig for answers, both uncover parts of their pasts that are best left buried. Not everything is as it seems, and they must figure out if their John Doe is connected to the secretive group that has moved onto the island. As facts materialize, danger on the island grows. Can Cassidy and Ty discover the truth about the shadowy crimes in their cozy community? Or has darkness permanently invaded their beloved Lantern Beach?

Attempt to Locate

A fun girls' night out turns into a nightmare when armed robbers barge into the store where Cassidy and her friends are shopping. As the situation escalates and the men escape, a massive manhunt launches on Lantern Beach to apprehend the dangerous trio. In the midst of the chaos, a potential foe asks for Cassidy's help. He needs to find his sister who fled from the secretive Gilead's Cove community on the island. But the more Cassidy learns about the seemingly untouchable group, the more her unease grows. The pressure to solve both cases continues to mount. But as the gravity of the situation rises, so does the danger. Cassidy is determined to protect the island and break up the cult . . . but doing so might cost her everything.

First Degree Murder

Police Chief Cassidy Chambers longs for a break

from the recent crimes plaguing Lantern Beach. She simply wants to enjoy her friends' upcoming wedding, to prepare for the busy tourist season about to slam the island, and to gather all the dirt she can on the suspicious community that's invaded the town. But trouble explodes on the island, sending residents—including Cassidy—into a squall of uneasiness. Cassidy may have more than one enemy plotting her demise, and the collateral damage seems unthinkable. As the temperature rises, so does the pressure to find answers. Someone is determined that Lantern Beach would be better off without their new police chief. And for Cassidy, one wrong move could mean certain death.

Dead on Arrival

With a highly charged local election consuming the community, Police Chief Cassidy Chambers braces herself for a challenging day of breaking up petty conflicts and tamping down high emotions. But when widespread food poisoning spreads among potential voters across the island, Cassidy smells something rotten in the air. As Cassidy examines every possibility to uncover what's going on, local enigma Anthony Gilead again comes on her radar. The man is running for mayor and his cult-like following is growing at an alarming rate. Cassidy feels certain he has a spy embedded in her inner circle. The problem is that her pool of suspects gets deeper every day. Can Cassidy get to the bottom of what's eating away at her peaceful island home? Will voters turn out despite the outbreak of illness plaguing their tranquil town? And the even bigger question: Has darkness come to stay on Lantern Beach?

Plan of Action

A missing Navy SEAL. Danger at the boiling point. The ultimate showdown. When Police Chief Cassidy Chambers' husband, Ty, disappears, her world is turned upside down. His truck is discovered with blood inside, crashed in a ditch on Lantern Beach, but he's nowhere to be found. As they launch a manhunt to find him, Cassidy discovers that someone on the island has a deadly obsession with Ty. Meanwhile, Gilead's Cove seems to be imploding. As danger heightens, federal law enforcement officials are called in. The cult's growing threat could lead to the pinnacle standoff of good versus evil. A clear plan of action is needed or the results will be devastating. Will Cassidy find Ty in time, or will she face a gut-wrenching loss? Will Anthony Gilead finally be unmasked for who he really is and be brought to justice? Hundreds of innocent lives are at stake . . . and not everyone will come out alive.

YOU MIGHT ALSO ENJOY ...

THE SQUEAKY CLEAN MYSTERY SERIES

On her way to completing a degree in forensic
science, Gabby St. Claire drops out of school and
starts her own crime-scene cleaning business. When a
routine cleaning job uncovers a murder weapon the
police overlooked, she realizes that the wrong person
is in jail. She also realizes that crime scene cleaning
might be the perfect career for utilizing her investiga-
tive skills.

#1 Hazardous Duty
#2 Suspicious Minds
#2.5 It Came Upon a Midnight Crime (novella)
#3 Organized Grime
#4 Dirty Deeds
#5 The Scum of All Fears
#6 To Love, Honor and Perish

HOLLY ANNA PALADIN MYSTERIES:

When Holly Anna Paladin is given a year to live, she embraces her final days doing what she loves most—random acts of kindness. But when one of her extreme good deeds goes horribly wrong, implicating Holly in a string of murders, Holly is suddenly in a different kind of fight for her life. She knows one thing for sure: she only has a short amount of time to make a difference. And if helping the people she cares about puts her in danger, it's a risk worth taking.

#1 Random Acts of Murder
#2 Random Acts of Deceit
#2.5 Random Acts of Scrooge
#3 Random Acts of Malice

THE WORST DETECTIVE EVER:

I'm not really a private detective. I just play one on TV.

Joey Darling, better known to the world as Raven Remington, detective extraordinaire, is trying to separate herself from her invincible alter ego. She played the spunky character for five years on the hit TV show *Relentless*, which catapulted her to fame and into the role of Hollywood's sweetheart. When her marriage falls apart, her finances dwindle to nothing, and her father disappears, Joey finds herself on the Outer Banks of North Carolina, trying to piece together her life away from the limelight. But as people continually mistake her for the character she played on TV, she's tasked with solving real life crimes . . . even though she's terrible at it.

ABOUT THE AUTHOR

USA Today has called Christy Barritt's books "scary, funny, passionate, and quirky."

Christy writes both mystery and romantic suspense novels that are clean with underlying messages of faith. Her books have won the Daphne du Maurier Award for Excellence in Suspense and Mystery, have been twice nominated for the Romantic Times Reviewers' Choice Award, and have finaled for both a Carol Award and Foreword Magazine's Book of the Year.

She is married to her Prince Charming, a man who thinks she's hilarious—but only when she's not trying to be. Christy is a self-proclaimed klutz, an avid music lover who's known for spontaneously bursting into song, and a road trip aficionado.

When she's not working or spending time with her family, she enjoys singing, playing the guitar, and exploring small, unsuspecting towns where people have no idea how accident-prone she is.

Find Christy online at:
www.christybarritt.com
www.facebook.com/christybarritt
www.twitter.com/cbarritt

Sign up for Christy's newsletter to get information on all of her latest releases here: **www.christybarritt. com/newsletter-sign-up/**

If you enjoyed this book, please consider leaving a review.

Made in the USA
Coppell, TX
27 April 2022

77137366R00156